The Carlin Trend

by

Tweed Jefferson

The Rockstar Nobody Series

Rockstar Nobody

The Carlin Trend

Freshman Nobody

Nobody Gets Out Alive

Music by The Walls Instead

Rockstar Nobody

Musicus Emeritus

Other Books by Tweed Jefferson

You Don't Look Artistic

Patrimonious

The Exceptional Musician

Jefferson, Tweed; The Carlin Trend

Fiction, Thriller | Fiction, Crime

ISBN 979-8-9898005-2-0

LCCN

Second Edition, 2024

First published in English in Junction City, Otegon

Again, for Katie

Contents

The Carlin Trend

Prologue

5150 an Essay

I should have never said anything. I knew better. Susan warned me.

The headaches have been getting worse lately. Well, they're not headaches so much, because it feels more like a void in my brain. It's not painful. The worst part is the memory loss. You know that feeling where you walk into a room and can't remember why you went in there? It's like that, except all the time. I can tell when it'll happen, too. My left eye goes blindingly white and I start to walk like back in my drinking days. I've affectionately named it the "Brain Hole".

I was about ready to put an actual hole in my head to make it go away. After a half-hour on hold with the suicide help line, I hung up and called my ex-wife. This is where I fucked up. She called the cops and they showed up at my door a couple of hours later to kidnap me at gunpoint. Well, assault-rifle point, technically.

So now I'm in the back of an ambulance on my way to the hospital. The medic is nice enough. I know a lot of these folks by name, but not by face, from my time as a 911 dispatcher. We share casual conversation during the hour-long trip down the mountain, neither of us mentioning why we're here in the first place.

I'm completely capable of walking, but they make me ride the gurney from the ambulance to the emergency room, then they lift me to a wheelie bed like I can't do it for myself. Expectedly, this hospital doesn't have any rooms available, so they roll my conveyance against a wall in the corridor, near the nurse's station. In the rooms on either side of me, patients scream and shout.

The security guard escorts me to the restroom at the end of the hall and has me strip naked with the door open. She gives me some paper scrubs, about six sizes too large, and a pair of brown hospital socks. My uniform for the weekend.

Before long, the nurse comes out from behind her desk and asks me a series of questions between jamming a thermometer in my mouth and pumping up a blood-pressure cuff.

"Are you hearing voices?"

"Are you thinking about hurting yourself or anyone else?"

"Do you have a plan?"

Regardless of what I'm thinking about, I know to answer these questions in the negative, otherwise they'll hold me hostage for longer than seventy-two hours or pump me full of meds. In this case, I followed Susan's advice. When she called me from this place, I think it was her second or third stay, we'd laugh about the irony of these so-called "mental health" facilities. They bring you in for thinking about suicide, then want to punish you for talking about it. If not here, where?

I attempt to count the dots in the acoustic ceiling tiles innumerable times to keep my mind active while waiting out my sentence. Every hour or so, the nurse does her same routine. At one point, they stick me in a room and a psychiatrist on a video monitor asks me the same questions. He doesn't seem to take my description of the Brain Hole seriously, either.

"What do you want us to do for you?" The nurse asks from behind the counter. I've lost all track of time and, of course, they have the clock facing in a direction where they can see it and I can't.

"I don't know, do some blood tests, have my head scanned? I want to know that what's happening isn't organic."

It's daylight again when the EMTs come to pick me up and haul me off to the next holding facility. I never did hear anything about getting those tests run. The last six months have been spent battling with my insurance company to see a specialist. No doubt they wouldn't make it easy on me this time around.

An orderly slams open the security door and beckons us inside. I sit complacently as the medics wheel me in on the gurney, waiting for permission to stand again. The man in the white scrubs takes my bag and, without bothering to look in it, shoves it into a locked closet with dozens of other suitcases, backpacks and plastic bags.

Past the second set of locked double doors a nurse stands behind a counter, watching patients pace the halls and talk to themselves. She escorts me to a small closet where she takes my blood pressure and other vitals. The equipment reads twenty-two respirations per minute. That is definitely wrong. I count my breath at about eight or ten per minute. Still faster than usual.

After another round of prosaic questions, she leads me to the room at the end of the hall, tells me which of the three beds is mine and closes the door, leaving me inside, in the dark. I flip the switch and the overhead fluorescents come to life like a thousand suns. There are blinds on the window, but they can't be opened. I decide to sit in the dark.

After several hours on the edge of my bed, staring into nothingness, a nurse comes to ask me, in a condescending tone, if I was planning to take my meds tonight. I don't typically take medication, so I'm not sure what they're planning to give me. I trek my way down the corridor and am given a paper cup with Ativan and my choice of either cran-apple or orange juice. She makes a note on her clipboard when I reject the juice in favor of water.

Before heading back to bed we all have to line up, shoulder-to-shoulder in the hallway to have our vitals checked. When it's my turn, the nurse asks the identical questions she asked when I came in:

"Why are you here?"

"I was thinking about hurting myself."

"Do you feel that way now?"

"No."

"Are you hearing voices?"

"No. I'm not schizo. I'm feeling depressed and have headaches." I learned at the last place not to refer to it as a "Brain Hole". It doesn't matter that the pamphlet they gave me when I got here said I had a *right* to medical treatment. Susan had the same problem. Near the end, she was almost unrecognizable. When her illness got worse, she couldn't eat and deteriorated rapidly those last couple of years. She told me that anytime she was feeling sick in here, they'd just send her to bed.

Tearing the Velcro band from around my arm, the nurse sends me back to my room for the night. The other two beds are now occupied. One roommate is fast asleep, the other is sitting bolt-upright on his bed, staring at the dark wall. I'm lucky to bunk with these guys and not whoever is screaming in the room across the hall.

There's an early-morning wakeup call and within five minutes I line up with the forty-or-so others in my ward and we march, single-file, to the cafeteria. Typically, I don't leave the house without a shower. I feel gross.

The nurse takes careful notes regarding what patients do, or don't, elect to take from the counter. The food is bland, burned and mostly-unidentifiable as real food. A lone lunch-lady denies additional portions of anything, but passes out dozens of packets of sugar, syrup or ketchup to each patient. I'm not a nutritionist, but I can't see how one egg, one piece of bread and some runny oatmeal, drowned in processed sugar, qualifies as a balanced meal. *"At least we aren't here for our health," he thinks sarcastically.*

After breakfast, we are allowed thirty minutes to clean ourselves. The three occupants of our room all manage to shower in the allotted time. After we clean ourselves, the nurses come around to take our soap, toothbrushes and mouthwash. They've made it clear that this will be our only opportunity to use any sanitary items until this time tomorrow. Are they afraid we'll try to eat the soap?

Before lunch, we have required exercise time. Once again, we line up way too close to each other and are marched down the hall to the 'gym'. I attempt to use one of the exercise bikes for a moment, giving up as the pedals spin freely. They're electric bikes, but the cords have all been cut. I grab a basketball from the rack and attempt to shoot it into the one hoop, against a far wall. It sticks between the rim and backboard, too flat to bounce. The other patients spin their wheels and dribble their flat balls. The atmosphere of the room makes me feel like if I don't pretend, I'll be punished.

They drive us like cattle back to our ward, only to immediately turn around and take us to the cafeteria. Lunch is more of the same. One dry chicken breast, one piece of bread, one iceberg wedge and all the ketchup, ranch dressing and sugar packets one can carry.

The daily calendar on the wall in my ward says there is a 'group' at three. Otherwise, no other activities are scheduled for today. Some patients choose to pace the halls or sleep, but most hang out in the common room, watching network TV and coloring with crayons. Seems like these are my only choices. I settle on Judge Judy and take a seat as far away from everybody as I can.

After seventy-three minutes of trash TV and staring at the clock, a nurse calls me into the closet to have my vitals checked again. She asks me the same questions as before. This time, I elaborate on the headaches and add some detail about having difficulty balancing while walking. I even throw in something about speech problems for good measure. The nurse removes the cuff and tells me to send in the next patient from the hall.

'Group' therapy consists of an hour of the most manic or delusional patients monopolizing the room by arguing with the indifferent social worker who sits at the head of a long table - or each other. Any hope for sharing or healing went out the door in the first thirty seconds and the counselor has no interest in reigning it in, dryly asking, “And how does that make you feel?”, no matter what delirious rant the patient would go on.

I won’t bore you with the details of dinner. Suffice it to say, every meal consisted of us lining up and being paraded down the halls to choke down what may as well have been cardboard, kitty litter and charcoal.

It’s been twenty-four hours. I still haven’t seen a doctor. The most medical attention I’ve received is having my blood-pressure checked. The most psychiatric care I’ve received was that Ativan.

I restlessly watch more network TV until what I’ve determined is the most appropriate bedtime to make myself look ‘normal’, which I decide is just after they offer me my ‘medication’.

This place is starting to get to me. Neglectful staff, bad food, no way to exercise our minds and bodies. It’s no wonder people come home from these places worse than when they left. If it weren’t for the pills, I don’t think I could sleep here. It’s everything that’s *not* home.

The next morning, after another round of questioning from the nurse and another unpalatable breakfast, I finally meet with a psychiatrist. She asks me the identical questions as the nurse. This time I elaborate even further on the headaches, not sure what notes the nurses have left in my file, if any. I tell her I have severe headaches, memory loss, vision and balance problems. Any individual with no medical training might suspect I had a stroke, the way I was describing the symptoms. All this so-called professional had to say before sending me back into the care of Judge Judy was, “It’s probably just depression. You can talk about it in group.”

This time, when we go to the gym, I only spend a couple

of minutes pretending to exercise on their broken equipment before joining a young woman sitting in the corner in playing with a giant Jenga set. I've tried to avoid interacting with other patients since I've been here, unsure why they are here and what might set them off. That's in addition to my general eschewal of any close contact with people. The nurses are watching and judging, so I make polite conversation with the girl as we play. She must be heavily medicated, not much of what she says makes sense. I can understand the words, just not the way she's putting them together.

For the rest of my stay, it's more of the same. The same questions from the nurses, with their same indifference to my care. When I meet with the shrink the next day, I'm crying, telling her I'm scared. That's no small feat for me. Despite being raised in a culture of toxic masculinity, I don't typically have any difficulty expressing the way I feel. Seldom, though, am I brought to tears. Her response is that if I don't stop being emotional, she'll keep me here past the seventy-two hours.

Monday morning I have an appointment with the man the staff refer to as the 'good doctor' (while simultaneously making racist jokes about the mean doctor within earshot of patients). Dr. Chaya tells me that I shouldn't be in this facility and I'm not getting appropriate care. He recognizes what I've had to say about the way things have been this weekend and all he can say is that he hears it a lot and wishes he could do something to change it.

After choking down my last terrible meal, they return my personal belongings and send me out the door. They don't ask if I have a ride home. All they provide me with is a paper with the phone number and address for the county health department, so I can "continue my care."

I probably won't. Not with them, at least.

My friend, Susan, tried to get help from the county. Before she died, she called every number she could find, from adult protective services to the sheriff. Nobody would help her. She said at one point that APS told her the fact she's able to call for herself must mean she's able to care for herself.

I spent just one weekend of my life being treated the way she, and many others, have been treated their entire lives. For one weekend, I didn't matter. I was less than a person. Completely helpless. In their ignorance, Susan's family kept encouraging her to go through the same torment, the same as my family has done to me. She hated doctors and hospitals, but all people could do was keep telling her to "get help". It's not all they could do; it was all they did. I don't know if I could have been the person to help her or not, but I know that there was no help, no healing, happening in the places they kept sending her.

Here I am, following in her footsteps. Lost, helpless, alone. But still alive.

Anhedonia.

That's me in a nutshell. I lived like this for almost two decades before I found out there was a word for it. For going through life feeling empty and meaningless, no matter what you do. If you've never heard it before, consider yourself fortunate. The meds make it worse. They always have.

I try. Try to make music. Try to cook. Try to work out. It all seems so pointless. I'm sick of trying.

There's a gun. I have one. I don't think I'd use it. I've always wanted to cut my belly instead. I'd need a 'second' if I'm going to do it right. Kaishakunin. Either way, I'm probably not going to do it today, just like I haven't done it the last six-thousand days that I've wanted to. I can't muster up enough energy and enthusiasm to kill myself. That's fucking irony.

Instead, I'll just do what I do every day: alternate between lying in bed, watching the walls, and working manically on my music. For a Libra, I lack balance.

I wonder if the samurai were always sick, too. In addition to living in a constant state of anxiety, they had pretty shitty diets most of the time, subsisting on rice and millet. Maybe they cut their bellies less as some righteous ceremony and more to release the demons that lived in there. That's how it feels to me. I used to think about poking holes in my abdomen in a desperate attempt to relieve the pain.

It's different now. I've always wanted to kill myself, but now it's more about not going out in some sterile hospital bed, surrounded by doctors and nurses who couldn't give a damn about me. I want to finish my projects. Like an epitaph. I could live a hundred years and not finish every project that lives in my head, so I've narrowed it down to a handful of the most important ones.

My phone buzzes. Carlin is excited for the next tour and texts me daily for updates. I was hoping to get this album released before committing to a bunch shows. Seems like there's always too much on my plate. Constantly teetering on burnout. This is why I quit touring when I turned thirty.

Being a musician, even an unsuccessful one, is hard work. It's romanticized to seem like we hang out at lavish parties with our instruments and begrudgingly accept the adoration of our fans. In reality, it's countless emails, phone calls and spreadsheets. Post-it notes and to-do lists everywhere. Don't forget about doing the same radio and print interviews over and over. And that's when we aren't rehearsing, writing or recording.

The problem is, in most bands, all of this work falls on one person. Until there's enough fame and fortune to hire out every task, the band is their own agent, manager, producer, accountant, lawyer, promoter, etc. Inevitably, due to my experience in management and production, I become the defacto do-everything-guy. Meanwhile, my band members keep asking for updates and paychecks for things they could certainly be helping out with. This current group of guys aren't so bad. Other bands, it feels more like babysitting than band-leading.

My own musical career has gone through at least four distinct phases. I've gone through twice as many personally, I'm sure. When I started playing in bands, it was all about being an artist and living the rock'n'roll lifestyle, never to be corrupted by things like cover songs and selling out. It's the most exciting approach to the business, with the biggest chance of a huge payoff – and the lowest chances for success. This is the version of the musician most people are familiar with.

After several years of starving in indie bands, I got into cover bands. Not just cover bands, epic tribute-band productions with cued lighting and costume changes and set design. The works. If I couldn't be creative with the music, I was determined to do it with the performance. It always amazes me to see the huge crowds that turn out for a Rolling Stones or The Doors tribute band. Not that there's anything wrong with that kind of music, but there are so many awesome independent artists out there working their asses off for crowds of half-a-dozen listeners. Meanwhile, next door, the overpriced microbrewery is at capacity with middle-aged married couples who would rather listen to the same fifty-year-old songs week-in, week-out, than ever experience something new. It's all about selling the comfort-zone. This is why the corporate radio stations play the same six hours of music over and over again. It's simply not offensive to anyone.

One thing about the cover bands, there's money in it. Not great money, and there never will be, but it's the easiest way to make a 'living' as a musician. If you can live on four or five hundred bucks a week. The constant gigging, playing the same songs every night, never growing as an artist, can be frustrating and exhausting, which is why I got into studio work.

I've studied popular music exhaustively for over two decades. Given the way I am, I probably don't listen to music like your average person – enjoying the lyrics, melody or overall feeling of the song. I analyze and memorize every note of every instrument, dissecting the arrangement and trying to understand the subtle nuance of how every note interacts with the next. Makes it hard to actually *enjoy* music or even use it as background noise when reading or writing. On the plus side, I've gained an understanding of mixing and arranging not available to your average musician.

The third phase of my music career was spent in the studio, both as a session player and producer. A lot of great records came out of that studio. Hundreds of songs in total. There was always one thing wrong with my records, though. I knew too much about music production and wanted to use all of the tools in my workshop. Instead of creating art through expression,

I mathematically determined the formulas for what would sell. And while it works commercially, it wasn't working artistically. Not for me.

Last year, thanks to my mental breakdown, I entered the most recent phase, a more genuine, honest approach to music. Like when I first started playing, I'm expressing myself again. Unlike when I first started, I'm doing it without looking for validation from anybody else. And while it may not be the most commercially-viable material I've ever released, I think I'm actually proud of it. I don't know what pride is supposed to feel like and if I'm supposed to feel guilty for having it. Either way, I think my latest project is objectively good and it actually has some power and meaning to it. Yet, it's simple – like nigiri sushi. I'm still too ashamed of myself to actually promote the album on my personal Facebook, but that probably has less to do with my music and more to do with my reticence at having any sort of interaction with people, however meaningful or trivial. Especially people from my past.

I message Carlin back and tell him to start looking for bands on our route who would be good to connect with. I don't have the time, or the motivation, to listen to dozens of local band demos. I doubt he'll want to do it, either, but I'd rather put him on a task so he can be involved in the planning of this tour instead of just texting me about it. I've been a little distracted with launching this website.

Instead of sifting through the endless stream of emails, I'm trying to set up a site where someone can post about the people who have hurt them. An online forum or classified, if you will. The design has been easy enough, but I still haven't figured out how to manage quality control. I would have to continue to read and approve every post to keep the trolls away unless I can figure out how to filter out the crap. That, or find a moderator to run things for me. But I don't know of anyone I can trust with this kind of project. Someone who understands that the resolution of these messages has to come from a place of healing, not a place of anger.

On top of all that, I've been converting my house into a full-blown recording retreat. Back when I was working in conventional studios, usually in the downtown or industrial area of a metropolitan city, I thought it would be awesome to be able to spend a week in a studio up in the mountains or out at the beach, alternating between focusing completely on the recording and relaxing in nature. When your band-mate is on their fiftieth take, trying to get that bass fill just right, it's nice to have somewhere to retreat. Most studios indie studios luxury extends as far as a shabby bathroom and, if you're lucky, a couch. Getting some distance from the session means going for a smoke in the alley. Now that I have this house up in the hills, I can make this dream a reality for other aspiring musicians and songwriters. The upstairs will stay bedrooms, while I'll expand the studio across the entire downstairs, using multiple rooms for isolation and acoustics. I'm not entirely sure how I feel about having a bunch of musicians staying in my house for weeks at a time, but as long as they don't trash the place, it'll be a good opportunity to make some killer records.

Too many projects can and will overwhelm me, but instead of being smart and just working on one at a time, I spend a lot of time bouncing around from task to task, not being able to focus. Alternating from pacing around the house to sitting outside with my coffee and cigarettes. Some days I only get an hour or two of actual work done. The memory loss makes it even more difficult. Sometimes, I'll finally get inspired to write or record and by the time I get into the studio, I've forgotten all of my theoretically-genius ideas. It's not something that's exclusive to just me, Tenacious D even wrote a song about it. Jimi Hendrix once said that even he couldn't get the sounds to come out of his guitar the way he heard them in his head. I think it was him. Either way, it's maddening. An endless supply of ideas and just one crazy person standing in the way of making them all a reality. I seriously need a handler. Someone to keep me on task, to bounce ideas off of. To make sure I eat.

I need a break from trying to force myself to be creative, so I run Lena around the yard with a ball on a rope. It's her favorite. I built it to be a practice kusarigama, but once she discovered it, it became a dog toy. She's almost as big as Mizu, but still has all the energy of a puppy. My little wrecking ball. I wish I had that kind of energy. After five minutes of running around, I'm tired and need to sit down. I don't always realize, at first, that I'm hunched over almost ninety-degrees in pain. Sorry, girl, I wish I were a better dad. That's the other thing about my handler, they need to love dogs how I love dogs. They'll be responsible for them after all this is over.

I remember when I was younger, reading Kurt Cobain's journals, and he talked about how heroin was the only thing that ever helped with his pain. This was back when my own stomach issues had just started. Ever since then, I've wanted to try it. It's not that I haven't had the opportunity. I've always been scared of needles, for one. To the point where I pass out when I have blood drawn. Tattoos were different. That kind of needle never bothered me. Getting my nipples pierced, that's its own story. I was a kid. Anyway, I don't usually do drugs any more. When I'm on the road, it's one thing, but I can't do them every day like I did in my twenties. My recovery time is too long. Shit, this bottle of whiskey has lasted almost a month. Every time I'm hurting like this, where I want to cut open my belly to relieve the pain, I think I should get some heroin. I might die, but I might feel better. Maybe it's not the heroin that inspired the great works of Brad Nowell, Shannon Hoon, and countless others, but the fact that they finally found enough relief from their pain to create the music that had been within them the whole time

As if there aren't enough orange and yellow sticky-notes on every surface of my house, I pull out the pad and start making yet another to-do list. Hopefully, it'll help get me on task for a couple more days while I sort out everything for this tour and album.

In the studio and on stage, I could very well be considered an expert of the segue, moving seamlessly from one section or song to the next. In regular life, I'm anything but. Struggling to transition from task to task or topic to topic. Either I'm too focused on the task at hand, never finding an appropriate stopping point, or I'm so distracted, I fixate on moving on to the next thing, mindlessly allowing my monkey-mind to run the show. That's how I'm feeling now.

These are the last two songs.

This is the hard part. Recording an album is a lot like being a gold-rush prospector. At first, there are nuggets sitting right on the surface: bright, shiny, and asking to be picked up. As the album progresses, there's more silt and crap to sift through before finding the smaller flakes. As the end of the record nears, you have to dig deeper and deeper, fracking thousands of tons of rock away before finding the vein that will make it all worthwhile. I'm digging deep now. I should have called this album 'Relode'.

At this point, if I can figure out what the hell I'm doing with Murder Hornettes and get one more vocal track from Carlin, I can start tying up the tracking for everything. I don't even really care what song he does. I had slated fourteen songs for this album, but with one more vocal song, that would make eleven. I'll shelve the other three until the next album. Or maybe forever. They aren't my favorites, anyway.

As always, before I can start work, I have to go around the studio with my ostrich-feather duster and clean the soot from everything. The whole state has basically been on fire for a couple months now and even with the windows closed, my house needs a dusting every couple of days to remove the burnt remnants of millions of trees – and the homes of a few poor souls. All of the equipment and furniture in my studio is black. I call it the Black Lab. Anymore, it's more like a chocolate lab, with speakers and monitors a chalky-brown. Slapping the sound foam panels that I have glued to the walls creates clouds akin to clapping together old chalkboard erasers in grade school.

It took about three months to get inspired to write the horn lines for Murder Hornettes. If you take into consideration the fact that I cut the rhythm tracks five years ago, it took much longer. Now, I just have to make up my mind whether to throw a couple hip-hop verses on it or make it an instrumental with dirty horn solos. I could dig it either way. Regardless, I have to lay down some Hammond organ tracks and maybe an epiano. Sadly, I got rid of my B3 years ago. It was too much of a hassle to move around and mic up. Now I just record my tracks through the keyboard and use patches to get the sounds I like. Virtual instruments have really improved the last few years. Most of them sound convincingly like real instruments, which makes life easier for me. Today, though, I won't even be playing the keyboard. This entire song, save for the bass and guitar, has all been written on the piano roll, and that's how I intend to finish it.

Before writing new parts, I write down all of the chords in the song and then each of the notes in that chord. It's already in my head, but when I write it down, I can score the piano roll at three or four times the speed. Go figure. Still not as fast as if I played the parts live, but more accurate, for sure.

Finishing the keyboard parts, I can't think of any other tracking I have left to do. Aside from a couple vocal tracks, I think I can officially move on to the mixing phase. My albums are typically done in overlapping stages, so as I'm tracking one song, I have others at various phases of mixing. Booze and Power Over, for example, were already mixed and released before we went out on the last tour. All they need is to be mastered with everything else.

The number one question I get asked is, "What's the difference between mixing and mastering?" They're similar but different. When I'm mixing a song, I take each of the individual tracks – the guitar, vocal, snare drum, violin, etc. - and first make them sound good by themselves. This means using effects like EQ and reverb to bring out the natural highlights in the tone of each instrument. As each track is sounding good on its own, I add in the instruments one at a time, adjusting the mix, EQ and effects to make one instrument sound complimentary to the next.

Once all of that is done, and every instrument can be heard at an appropriate level, countless passes of listening through different speakers and making minuscule, nearly inaudible, changes to the mix occur. Finally, we have a song. However, that song still isn't ready for the public. This is where the mastering process starts. If it's going on an album, each of the songs will need to be mixed in comparison to each other so they will have a consistent volume and attitude throughout the album. This is also the time to arrange the song order and put transitions between songs into the fold. And, finally, once all of that is done, we give each song one last treatment of EQ, reverb and limiting to create an appropriate volume and frequency for play on radio and streaming outlets.

"Hey dude, send me your tracks," I text Carlin.

"Sorry. I'll do it today or tomorrow."

While I wait on those last tracks, I decide to remix Rockstar Nobody, the title track from the album. I am not happy with the mix. With the song in general, really. At the same time, I don't want to, or don't think it's necessary to, retrack any parts. I *should* be able to make what I have sound good.

Yoshi, forever my sidekick, lays on the leather couch in the studio, obviously as bored with listening to this song over and over again as I am. He and Charlie are getting old. I was hoping I could hold out longer than them. Especially Yoshi. He's the Hachiko-type that would sit and wait for me to come back. That idea fills me with more sadness than anything I've ever known. People forget about us with haste. Our dogs never do.

He's up now. Leaping from the couch, barking like a psycho. The other three are outside, going nuts as well. Usually, it's a squirrel, but I can tell by the timbre of their voice that something else is going on. I save my project and find my shoes.

"Guys, yame. Hush."

There's a tow truck attempting to make its way up my washed-out gravel driveway, slipping and banging as the dogs run alongside, barking ferociously. There's no way that truck will be able to turn around up by the house. I run down the driveway and wave at the driver to stop. He rolls down his window.

"I have a delivery here for...I can't read the name." He flips his clipboard over to show me a bill of lading. I didn't order anything. Obviously, I want it, though. I tell him to unload in the flat spot down by the gate while I lock the dogs in the house.

I lift the gull-wing door and take a look inside. Brand new. It only has eighty-eight miles on it. There's an envelope on the passenger seat. A Thanksgiving card. The only other time I've received a Thanksgiving card, it was from this massage therapist pretending to be a doctor. He needs to go on the list, for sure. Not only did he cheat me out of paying for the work I did for his 'school', he's duped countless students into thinking he's a legitimate medical professional. Manipulating naive, young girls into sleeping with him by pretending he has some sort of secret to enlightenment. A wannabe cult-leader is what he is.

I can't thank you enough for what you did to help me. There's no way I could ever repay you, but maybe this will be a start. Come see me next time you're on the road!

xoxo, Taryn

Quite a different kind of Thanksgiving than I'm used to. I get to play with my dream car and, so far, no animals have had to die. Sucks that I still can't drive much. That's not going to stop me from taking this thing for a test drive. She couldn't possibly know what I *actually* did for her, right? I never heard anything about that night again. Either she has a suspicion, or somehow she thinks driving her around in an RV for a week is worth a new car. I doubt it. Either way, this is the first time in my life that karma has actually worked in my favor. It's a welcome change from always letting myself be taken advantage of. Taryn could have never talked to me again, having gotten what she needed.

She's the one with real integrity.

Sorry, doggos, it's a two-seater, so I'm taking this ride solo. These aren't the most powerful cars and it doesn't do great over the hills, but handles the curves down the mountains with ease. There's an irony to my love for this car. I don't like to be the center of attention, even on stage, but I've always wanted this car, even knowing that everyone will point it out and ask about it. That's not why I wanted it. Actually, it seems like a great reason for me to not want a car like this. I've always preferred something practical and nondescript. A Corolla or Jetta or a minivan. Probably meet a lot more girls with a car like this.

It's not like meeting girls is hard when you're a musician, but there's rarely any kind of connection. I don't have much patience for the superficial and vapid. I could connect with anyone if I tried, but the hard part is finding someone who can accept and love all of my interests and idiosyncrasies. My flaws. No matter how much someone says they love music, there's always a breaking point when it comes to my obsession with it. My obsession with everything, really. I imagine it can be exhausting just to watch. I run myself to critical mass, then spend a few days in bed, which they also find frustrating. Being with an artist can be exciting at first, I'm sure, but after a while, they all want me to be "normal". And after another while, I try to be normal. Going through the motions of what we've been raised to believe is life. Following these rules that we're told are essential to our happiness. And after that while, I go crazy because I've forgotten about the artist in me and it's fighting to get out. It's a regular cycle. I'm doomed to either repeat it or be alone.

Interestingly enough, as I've experienced this cycle over the past couple decades, I've noticed something else. I seem to have the Good Luck Chuck curse. If you want to call it a curse. Everyone I've been in a relationship with has, in their very next relationship, found true love and gotten married. Well, I can't say that it's true love, but they have all gotten married. I don't know what that says about me. I'm awesome or terrible, I suppose. Either they settle for the next 'normal' guy they meet or they decide that they won't, or don't want to, find another person quite as, shall we say, dynamic as me. I have noticed that these future husbands are all the anti-creative, working-stiff, sitcoms-at-night, football-on-weekends type of guys. The complete opposite of me. I'll never be able to fully psychoanalyze why this has happened over a dozen times so far. Maybe it's some supernatural force. I'm cursed. Or Blessed. I could use my powers for good if I weren't so damn selfish.

The album is done by Christmas. Not that the release date matters much anymore. Here in the twenty-first century, it would be a rare pre-teen who would wait excitedly on Christmas morning to unwrap a new record. Especially one of ours.

Once the album comes out, the messages pour in, often without even mentioning our music. This is the kind of stuff I was hoping to figure out how to filter. More people wanting to take advantage with no intention of giving anything back. This system will never work unless we all help each other.

My husband is such a piece of shit. I just caught him cheating on me for the third time. He doesn't give a shit about me or our kids...

That sucks, lady, but what do you expect me to do about it? I guess I'm available for a revenge fuck? Delete. Lots of messages about affairs. I'm tempted to do a keyword search and delete them all.

I was fired from my job so they could hire the manager's cousin. I did nothing wrong and now, with the way the economy is, I'm not going to be able to find another job...

I don't know if this guy is asking for money, a job or for retaliation against his boss. Delete. I can see most of these messages have been read already.

Fuck the police. ACAB. We should take them all out. Kill all those fucking pigs...

Uh, I agree? How am I supposed to respond to these messages? Write back and tell them that the best way to do it would be to unify the street gangs and, at a predetermined date and time, spread out into the small towns across the state, walking into substations to file fake reports, then opening fire when they sit down to take your information? Chaos in the rural areas would disrupt coverage in metropolitan areas, as resources are sent to remote areas of the state, allowing the gangs to then return to the cities and take control of the understaffed police departments. Not just the gangs, all allies in the fight against fascism. Obviously, I would never say something like that out loud.

"Hey, those messages are getting crazy," Carlin says, sitting in the wicker chair across from me on the patio. We're having a little band get-together to celebrate the release of the album. Having a release party at a club is pretty much out of the question right now.

"Yeah, man, I know. That's what I get for inviting people to write to us, I guess."

"I don't think the other guys would agree, but I can't get over the idea that we should be doing something to help."

"I've been thinking about that a lot. I just can't figure out how to filter out all the crap. You've seen it. I don't want us, or anybody else, doing anything stupid just because someone is mad at their boyfriend."

"We can't go through them all, I know. Let's say we just pick one or two?" He passes me his phone, already open to a particular message.

Dear The Walls Instead,

My name is Anastasia Wallace. I'm fourteen years old. The nurses say I'm too young to be listening to your music, but I do it anyway. The nurses say a lot of things. Especially one nurse, Lydia. She tells us that it's our fault we're sick. That God is punishing us for our sins and the sins of our families. I haven't seen my parents or sister in over three months. They say it's because of Coronavirus, but I don't think it's right that they get to go home every night to see their families and we're left here alone. Lydia says we're never going home and that if we would just hurry up and die, they could use the beds for people who actually need them. I read about how you were in the hospital and they wouldn't help you either. Is this how it is everywhere? Can I use your music in my video diaries?

Love, Anastasia

"You told her she could, of course?"

"Of course. But could we do something else? Break her out or at least get that nurse fired?"

"Stealing a child from a hospital might be a little extreme, but I'm down to do something. Start doing your research. Anything and everything you can find on this nurse."

The glass door slides open behind Carlin. Chris and Simon pass out a round of beers and fill in around the table.

"Oh shit, THC vodka? Can I have a shot?" Chris asks, eyeing the plastic bottle that I've drawn a huge skull-and-crossbones on in sharpie.

"Yeah, go for it, but no promises as to what will happen. I've never tried it straight."

Carlin flips over a cocktail glass and pours a double over some ice. Edibles make me tired, so I abstain. Hopefully these guys won't be passing out all over my house thirty minutes from now.

“Congrats on the album, mate.”

“Thanks, brother. Thanks to all you guys for being a part of it.”

“So what’s the plan for the next tour?”

“I’m still ironing everything out, but we’re heading north. Portland, Seattle, San Francisco and the like. With the clubs starting to reopen, we’ll probably do a mix of venues and underground shows.”

“Right on, man,” Chris says. “I did that route last year. No. Shit, two years ago now. Should be fun. And cold!”

“Yeah, let’s hope we don’t get snowed in, like last time I was up there.”

“Fuck that, man. I don’t want to drive that big-ass RV in the snow.”

“It’s all freeway, we should be fine. Like you ever drive anyway!”

“That’s a nice ride you’ve got down at the bottom of the hill. Finally getting paid for those videos?” Simon asks, changing the subject.

“Not really. It was a gift from a fan, believe it or not. May as well belong to all of us. You guys are welcome to borrow it. I can’t do a whole lot of driving lately, anyway.

“I was thinking about hiring a road manager so we don’t have to worry about driving so much this trip. You guys know anyone?”

“What about Jesse?” Chris offers.

“Uh, I could be down to have him go with us…if he can stay sober long enough to drive from gig to gig. That’s kinda the whole job.”

“Yeah, good point. You know he’ll say he will, but once the rest of us start drinking, he’s not going to want to be left out.”

“We may as well give him the chance.”

Packed and ready to go.

Since we just had the RV out a couple of months ago, it takes no time at all to get it ready for the next trip. I still haven't been able to get the ice maker to work. Aside from that, I've got us all stocked up on beer and snacks. Time to get this show on the road.

First stop is Carlin's. Fortunately, he doesn't have much to bring with him, just his faded-blue duffel bag. It's fortunate because I can't pull the RV into his neighborhood, with its single-lane, one-way roads lined with parked cars on either side. It's a pain to drive my regular car in there.

"Dibs on the loft this time," he says, tossing his bag above my head.

"Fuck that. You know your drunken ass isn't going to want to hobble up that ladder every night."

I drop the rig into gear and head out toward the main road, looping the neighborhood to avoid having to make a u-turn against traffic. The sun is already starting to go down, so I flip on the headlights. Damn, I was hoping to get to Jesse's before dark.

We've just rounded the second corner when Carlin yells out for me to stop. I slam on the brakes and skid to a halt in the middle of the neighborhood. He hops out of the seat and leaps from the door, the steps still retracted.

"Hey! What are you doing? Stop that!" He shouts into a neighboring yard. I lean across the passenger seat to see who he's talking to. Behind the chain-link fence, a Fresno Sheriff's deputy is dragging a bloodied young woman by her hair across the dead, yellow grass.

"Fuck off, man. This is a private matter. Get back in your vehicle and get the fuck out of here!" He tells back at Carlin from across the sidewalk. The woman is crying and begging for help under the grip of the deputy. She grasps her hair to prevent him from tearing any more of it out. He outweighs her by an easy two-hundred pounds, his greasy skin shimmering under the streetlights as they flicker on. The back of his shaved head looks like a pack of hot dogs, ready to burst in the microwave. His swastika tattoo must be hidden under the uniform.

"No way, dude, I'm not going to leave and let you do whatever the fuck this is."

The cop pulls out his gun and points it at Carlin, losing his grip on the woman. She makes a break for it and runs barefoot down the street. The fat pig holsters his weapon and gives chase, shoving Carlin to the ground as he waddles through the gate.

From my position next to the door, I leap back into the driver's seat and floor it, chirping the tires as the rig falls into drive. The deputy is only a few feet in front of me when I gain traction. His three-hundred pounds are no match for the three tons of my camper. I pass over him without resistance. Barely a bump. When I see his motionless body by the back wheels in my mirror, I hit the brakes.

"Body cam!" I yell at Carlin as he rushes back to the cabin door, still open. He circles around the back, crawling between the back tires, and returns holding the little black box. The woman has turned a corner and is nowhere in sight. Just as well, we can't stick around here long. The death-squad is going to be showing up soon. The back tires thump imperceptibly over the incapacitated deputy as we head north towards the highway.

"Fuck, dude! What the fuck was that?" Carlin pants as he slams the door closed and makes his way back to the cockpit.

"I don't know. Fuck that guy. He pulled a gun on you, man."

"Shit, now what are we going to do? They're going to be looking for us."

"Maybe. But we're on our way out of town. Did you see

any witnesses?"

"Just the lady. Do you think it was his wife?"

"No telling. Could be. Fresno cops are known for being wife-beaters. But they're also known for giving out beatings to people for looking at them wrong, so we may never know what set that asshole off this time."

We sit in silence for the rest of the ride to Jesse's. He's obviously on edge. Let's hope this doesn't put a damper on the tour.

The guys meet us outside as we pull up in front of Jesse's house.

"Whoa, what the heck happened?" Jesse asks, pointing at the broken headlight as I shut the engine off.

"Hit a deer on the way down the hill. We're going to have to fix that tomorrow. Got a hose?" He drags a coil of garden hose from the flower bed and sprays the blood off the front bumper and grill.

"What the fuck, man?" I say, pointing to the beer in his hand. With this diversion, I snatch the ragged piece of tan fabric from behind the battered chrome bumper and shove it in my pocket.

"It's my first one, I swear." I look over at Chris and he shrugs and nods, as if confirming he's only seen him have the one since he's been here. I don't really give a shit about Jesse drinking while we're on the road, I just don't want him to be getting blackout drunk. He and I are the same like that; we don't know how to turn it off. One of my favorite stories about him is the time he, Chris and I were in a band together and he puked a soup of Fireball, Modelo, and Little Caesars all over his congas at the end of our closing song. Totally epic finale.

It seems like we have *way* more gear this time, as we load out drums and speakers from Jesse's living room and into the basement of the RV.

"Where's your throne, man?"

"Oh, snap! Thanks for reminding me." Chris runs back into the house and emerges with the faux-leather stool. Jesse loads his congas, even though I told him we weren't set up for him to perform with us on this trip.

A silver Prius pulls into the driveway, the hatchback flopping wildly over the padded keyboard case that's sticking out over the rear bumper. Simon hops out of the passenger seat and wheels the gig bag from the Prius over to the rig.

"What's up, fellas?" He greets us as he makes another trip across the driveway to get his suitcase. "Ready to do this thing?"

"Fuckin-A, let's hit it!"

We say our goodbyes to Jesse's family and pile into the bus. I text Spiderweb, our host for the first part of the trip, and let him know we're on our way.

"You can have a pass tonight," I tell Jesse as I climb past him and into the driver's seat. I don't need to tell him twice. He's already heading for the fridge. Only three hours until our first stop. Night driving sucks, but I should be able to handle it. It's only one freeway the whole time.

"You want a beer, bro?" Chris passes a can up to the front and I empty it into my Taco Bell cup. "How you feeling? Sure you can drive?"

"No worries, man. I'm fine." The headaches haven't been so bad lately. I asked the McDoctor to change my meds and he refused, so I stopped taking them. It helped quite a bit with the headaches. I still get sick a lot. The neurologist thinks this all could have been caused by a head injury from twenty years ago and it's just starting to manifest now. Still, nobody knows how long until it gets so bad I can't function. Could be five years, could be tomorrow. On the good days, I feel like it could be the former. On the bad days, I'm certain it will be the latter.

Chris offers me a bump from his car key, but I decline. These guys don't know Spiderweb. The next day-and-a-half with him is going to be non-stop. I need to preserve my heart-rate as long as I can. I do accept the joint from Carlin and take a few puffs before passing it back and hitting the signal lever as I turn onto the freeway on-ramp.

Ugh. The 99 corridor. Hundreds of miles of barren wasteland, smog, and abandoned marquees. On the bright side, when the apocalypse comes, everyone who lives in the valley will already be used to it. We'd barely even notice as long as the drive-thrus stay open. California is a beautiful state, as long as you keep yourself fifty miles to either side of this deadly freeway. It's not the road itself, it's wide, flat and straight. It's the drivers. I don't know why, but this freeway is like a magnet for idiots.

"What's the deal with rooms this time around?" Simon asks, putting his feet up on the couch and pulling on his sunglasses as he lounges back.

"Well, we're staying with Spiderweb tonight, you guys already know. I booked rooms almost every night, except the nights we're driving. The itinerary is in the kitchen, if anyone wants to get any additional rooms or anything."

"I'm cool just staying in the RV, man," Chris says.

"Same here," Jesse agrees.

After a quick stop in Modesto for gas and liquor, we're back on the dreaded never-ending highway. It's putting me to sleep. Luckily, it isn't much longer before we're pulling off the freeway in Sacramento.

"Shit, I forgot about the parking in this neighborhood." I loop around the one-way streets, searching for anywhere appropriate to leave something this size overnight. Eventually, I pull under the freeway, only a block away from Spiderweb's house.

"Aren't you worried about the bums?"

"You guys gotta check this out. Get whatever you need for tonight." Everyone grabs their bags and waits outside, under the massive concrete ceiling of the overpass. I pull the cord for the sunshade and a corrugated aluminum sheet rolls out over the side of the RV, covering the doors and windows.

"That's bad-ass, man."

"Yeah, I figured we never use the shade-cloth, right?" I reach under the wheel-wells and secure the straps to their locking mechanisms.

The little plastic wheels on Simon's suitcase bounce frantically on the broken pavement and gravel under the freeway. Thankfully, he picks the bag up and carries it. Until we make it back to the sidewalk, at which point it begins bouncing and creaking over the cracks in the cement.

Spiderweb lives in this old Victorian mansionette right in the middle of the city, surrounded by freeways and commercial high-rises. It's a trip.

"Well, would you lookie what we have here," Spiderweb says, chuckling, as he opens the glass-paned front door, letting the band pass by. "Good to see you, brother."

His beard has gotten long and scraggly since I've last seen him. He's lost some weight, too. Probably hasn't cut back on the drinking and partying. We spent countless nights drinking, doing drugs, shooting the shit until the sun came up. Long, crazy nights. It's interesting how I remember them more as an atmosphere of events than individual days and nights. How long has it been, anyway? Eight, nine years? Fuck, we're old.

"What's up, brother? Thanks for letting us crash your house like this. Have anything planned for us tonight?"

"Yuuuuuup," he burps. The putrid stench of his dinner and pale ale fills my nostrils.

Spiderweb takes us on a walking tour of midtown Sac, stopping at various brewhouses to sample their ales, which he insists are better than anything in Fresno. I don't disagree, Fresno beer is terrible. A rich bouquet of piss, sweat and vomit, buried in an overabundant bitterness of hops. If you're lucky. By the time we're at the third bar, I switch to cocktails so I don't have to stomach another disgusting IPA. I'd order a regular beer, if they had it, but I'm worried they'd ring a bell or some other stupid ritual they do at breweries to shame people for ordering beer that tastes more like water than urine.

Simon, Carlin, and I find a quiet table out on the patio and settle in while we wait for the other three to make their rounds through the bar, talking up the locals.

"These blokes gonna get us in trouble the first night out?"

"Eh, probably," I laugh. "Spiderweb has always been a bit of a wildcard."

"Why do you call him Spiderweb, anyway?"

"Fuck if I know, man. We were playing in a band with like four guys with the same name in it, so everyone got a nickname. I don't know where his came from. I think Kyle made it up."

Jesse and Spiderweb each bum a smoke from Chris as they step out onto the patio. Spiderweb, cigarette dangling from his lips, puts his arm around me as he sits down, his beer sloshing onto the table and into my lap.

"It's so good to see you, brother. I missed you." I never know how to react to these shows of affection. It happens a lot and every time, I feel uncomfortable. For one, I don't trust that it's genuine. Maybe right now, highlighted by a night of malt hops, it feels honest, but I know better. I think the people who really mean that sort of thing don't say it.

"What's up with your new band? Do we get to meet them?" His group is opening up for us tomorrow night. Well, kinda. I'm not sure how they're going to put together the show for tomorrow. It's not your typical music show.

"Nah, not tonight. Family shit. Let's go check out this other band, though."

We finish our drinks and set off on foot to a crumbling, graffitied, two-story building that looks like it could have once contained offices or studio apartments. Purple and green lights flash through the windows, illuminating the hordes of young white kids, dressed all in black, standing out front. We weave our way through the sea of patchouli and denim to the door, where Spiderweb gives a handshake and a hug to the door guy, then points at us. Nodding in turn to the bouncer, we make our way up the concrete steps and through the front door.

I could tell before we came in that I was not going to dig this place. Now that I'm inside, I'm certain. The entire building is separated into just two rooms, upstairs and downstairs. Downstairs, in the room we're standing in, there appears to be a rave or similar sort of event. I've never been a raver, so I don't know what kind of criteria must be met to qualify as a rave. This party has loud techno music, flashing lights and sweaty dancers.

The guys start to take a lap around the room, making their way to the bar. I can't handle it, so I beeline up the stairs to the second floor. Supposedly, this is the rock venue. Carlin notices and follows behind.

"Wait up, I'm slow." It's only like seven more steps to the bar, so I don't wait up. I don't think he's going to have any trouble finding me.

Thankfully, this room is nearly empty. There's a band on the stage, sucking loudly at an empty dance floor and a couple tables of what are clearly their girlfriends. I can't tell if this is a real venue or not. Like, licensed to operate and sell alcohol. Not that I'd care. The bar has canned and bottled beer. No taps. No cocktails. At least I can get a domestic beer without being singled out.

The rest of our entourage stumbles their way up the steps and fan out around the bar. Spiderweb leans in too close and shouts in my ear.

"See, I told you these guys were good!"

"Dude, these guys suck. If rumble were tone and yelling were melody, yeah, they'd kick ass." I'm trying to shout over the incredible din, but he isn't paying attention anyway. He peels himself from the bar and makes his way to the empty dance floor to stand in front of the stage and shout encouragement at the band. He's become one of *those* guys, apparently.

The noise is starting to get to me, so I make my way downstairs and back outside, through the crowds of smoking teens, and into the dirt alleyway beside the building. Anxiously, I smoke cigarette after cigarette and play with my phone, pretending to text, for what seems like an hour until the guys come out to look for me. I'm having a hard time picturing their faces. It happens sometimes. Part of the memory loss. I'm pinching the bridge of my nose with my thumb and index finger when Chris pokes his head around the corner.

"Dude, c'mon. Tacos!"

Around the next corner is a little shack with a line of the same smoking kids standing out front. The line moves fast. When we get to the counter, Spiderweb orders us twenty tacos and we stagger outside to wait for our food with the black-clad masses. When our number is called, Spiderweb announces that we're going back to the house of some dude he just met while we were waiting for our food, to eat tacos and drink beer. That last stop burned me out for the night, but I don't have a choice, I'm his guest. I can't exactly say that I'm going to bail and head back to his place. I mean, I could, but I won't.

The cramped basement apartment is decorated in mismatched thrift-store sofas and bean-bag chairs, each occupied by a glassy-eyed twenty-something, smoking blunts or playing video games. Those without their eyes fixated on a TV screen are poking at their phones. An opium den for a new generation.

I eat a couple of asada street-tacos as quickly as possible while standing against an empty wall, then begin gathering up our posse. Our unified intent to leave will surely get Spiderweb to walk us home. Or so we think. He's taken one of the only girls at this so-called party hostage and isn't letting her break away, as he stands less than a foot away from her, shouting into her face at a volume that might have been appropriate at the bar, but not here.

Her back is already against the wall. She keeps eyeing around either side of him, looking for a route of egress.

While Spiderweb is focused on taking advantage of this girl who is undoubtedly half his age, Simon slips something in his drink. He notices me notice him. I glance around the room and everyone else seems preoccupied with their own high.

Normally, I'd have a problem with someone roofying another person, but given the fact that if we left Spiderweb unattended, he'd probably do the same to this girl. I never actually saw him do it back in the day, but I have no doubt that he took advantage of several young women. Whether through actual date-rape drugs or conventional drugs and alcohol, he'd definitely use something as part of his courting ritual.

Eventually, we get sick of trying to get his attention and make our way outside, the claustrophobia having got the best of us. Simon and I can rest easy knowing that in a few minutes we can make our way back in and drunk-walk Spiderweb home.

"You have some interesting friends, my dude."

I'm the first up in the morning.

Creeping my way down the stairs, trying not to wake the unconscious masses spread out across the living room, I ease the oversized front door open and head up the street on foot. According to my map, there's an O'Reilly's or Pep Boys around here.

A couple of screws and twenty minutes later, the headlight is replaced and working. I walk back around the corner from the alleyway in time to see Chris and Carlin emerge from the house onto the porch, shading their eyes from the sunlight bouncing off the windows across the street as they light their morning cigarettes.

"Damn, dude, you must've got up hella early today."

"Eh, not that bad. We can't be getting pulled over in that rolling pharmacy."

"For sure. Spiderweb wants to take us to breakfast. Get cleaned up, I'll get the uber."

The breakfast joint is small and minimalist. I can appreciate the paper menu with only a dozen or so items on it and no pictures. I order the lox and bagels. Another one of those things I can never get at home and can't resist. That's twice in twelve hours that I've eaten meat. Bad influences around here. Spiderweb sends his eggs benedict back three times, first because the eggs aren't runny enough, then because they are too runny. I can never send food back. If it's a chef, I feel like I should eat the food the way they prepare it. If it's a cook, they'll probably spit in it. Or add some special sauce.

"So what's up with this gig tonight?"

"Oh, man, you guys are going to love it! We're the backing music for a burlesque show," Spiderweb says, chuckling. This dude is always either laughing as he speaks or shouting like he's in a wind tunnel.

"Cool!" Carlin exclaims. "I've always wanted to do that." I was a little concerned he might not take too kindly to giving up the spotlight. The band is used to playing in the background, but one never knows about the singer. I've known more than a couple singers who need to be front-and-center, even during guitar solos or instrumental tunes. Carlin isn't like that, but Spiderweb is. Maybe he'll get himself in trouble – again.

After a two-hour, European-style breakfast with plenty of coffee and breaks for cigarettes, we head back to the RV and take it across town to the venue. Like always, especially in downtown areas, parking sucks. We have to leave the rig idling in the street while we try to frantically unload our gear and haul it down the steps to the concrete patio, piling it haphazardly amongst the tables and chairs that have been padlocked to the bike racks overnight.

It's a cool little underground joint. Dimly lit, low ceilings. Perfect for a burlesque show. It's a bit too long and narrow for a music venue, but we aren't trying to blow the doors off the place. They have us set up our equipment over in the corner, to the side of the stage. Presumably, the dancers will be using all of the available floor space. Soundcheck is quick and easy. Since it's not a full rock show, we don't bother to mic up the drums and amps.

With a few hours to kill before doors open, we venture back to the street and wander our way into Old Town to find a drink. There's an old-timey piano bar around here somewhere, if I remember right. Doorknobs and window frames painted in faux-patina make a novelty of the city's desperate attempt to feel historical. Instead of *being* historical.

We find the saloon and saddle up to the bar for beer and whiskey. This room wasn't designed for acoustics. Each voice reflects around the room like a hall of mirrors. Once we get our drinks, I head outside for the sake of my ears. Not a moment too late, as the guys start racking up some balls for a game of pool.

I'm snubbing out my cigarette in the ashtray and contemplating the merits of going inside for a refill versus subjecting myself to the inevitable noise when Carlin comes through the door.

"Hey, check this out," he says, handing over his phone and pulling out the chair next to me.

Sheriff's Deputy Injured in Hit-and-Run

Fresno County Deputy James White is in critical condition after he was run over by an unidentified vehicle in front of his home on Friday night. The only known witness, the victim's wife, refuses to cooperate with authorities, stating that she was saved from White by the unknown assailants.

White, a twenty-one-year veteran of the force, had been implicated in domestic violence and sexual abuse cases several times in the past, each time, the responding officers refusing to file charges. Department records indicate White had seven complaints for excessive use of force in the previous twelve months, with no internal investigation launched. In light of this information, the Department of Justice has launched a full inquiry into both the Fresno Police Department and Fresno Sheriff's Department regarding their internal investigation and audit processes.

Any witnesses with information about last night's hit-and-run are asked to contact the Fresno Sheriff's Department.

"You feel better, man?"

"Yeah, a little bit. It actually feels good now, like we did something to change the future for a lot of people. For the better."

"For sure, I agree." Thinking long and hard about what I say next, I eke out, "So, about those messages…"

"I get it, bro, I see what you're doing with the tour

schedule. Kinda gave it away when you booked that gig in Yakima," he chuckles.

"There needs to be a few rules."

"Totally. The vigilante's code. The code is what separates a monster from a tool of good."

"Yeah, but I mean, mostly so we don't get caught. And don't fuck with kids and animals. That's my personal rule."

"Like you even need to tell me that," he says, pulling a folded piece of notebook paper from his jacket pocket and passing it to me. Details on the Yakima nurse. Her shifts, home address, vehicle type.

"Damn, dude, good job!" We won't have a lot of time in Yakima to scout things out, so we spend the next few minutes brainstorming how we're going to do it until it's time to interrupt the pool game indoors and lead everyone back to the venue.

We alternate two-song sets with Spiderweb's band, which is nice because we get to keep our drinks full and watch the show. Half of it, at least. This is a pretty legit burlesque show. I've been to a few before, but they were the local, make-middle-aged-women-feel-good-about-themselves type of burlesque show. This show features professional dancers. My favorite act, though, is the fat dude who does the Chris Farley Chippendale's dance. I'm glad I didn't get stuck trying to cop that Loverboy riff. So much of this gig is by the seat of our pants and we weren't given any material to rehearse. I guess the theory is, between the band and the dancer, we'll find *something* that will work for both of us.

The patio is crowded when Chris and Jesse start hauling gear between the tables and up the stairs. No back door at this venue. Simon pulls up in the RV and idles on the street in front of the club. With the help of Spiderweb's band, we get our gear out of the bar and into the storage compartment in about five minutes.

"Party at Chris Farley's house, dude," Chris says as he makes his way into the cabin. A band bus parked in front of a venue always gathers more attention than I'd like and several of the audience members from the show are attempting to make their way in. Carlin is the last one on board and we manage to get out of there with only a couple of stowaways.

Chris Farley, whose name is actually David, lives just down the street from the venue in a residential neighborhood that, amazingly, has available street parking. Simon pulls up to the curb a few houses down and we pile out onto the grassy verge.

After the 'party' we went to last night, this is a welcome reprieve. Adults interacting instead of stoner kids in a basement, staring at screens. The performers from tonight's show are spread out around the rooms of the house, leaving plenty of space to walk around or find a seat by myself. Buttoning my jacket and flipping my collar, I go out back and take up residence on the old baby-blue sofa on the porch.

"You gonna stay out here?" Chris asks, he and Carlin shivering between hits on the glass pipe that I gave him like three years ago during one of my many attempts to quit smoking.

"Just for a smoke or two."

Carlin opens the back door and waits, holding it, as one of the dancers from the show comes out, fishing a cigarette from the pack in her coat pocket. He and Chris check her out from behind before making their way back inside. She sits down next to me on the couch and puts her feet up on my lap.

"Bum a light?" I search in my jacket for the lighter for a moment, before lighting her cigarette. "You guys are good."

"Oh, thanks. You, too." We backed her up, so I actually didn't see much of her act. The audience seemed to dig it. She wore a blue and black bikini and did a food thing, rubbing chocolate sauce and whipped cream on herself and the like. We played Dirty Work by Steely Dan for her act. She's cleaned up now, clad in yoga pants and a sweatshirt under her gray, woolen peacoat.

She's not from here. Santa Barbara. They're a group of touring burlesque performers who team up with local dancers for shows like these. I didn't know that was a thing. I mean, everything is a thing, but I've never heard of a touring burlesque act before. She goes by Phoenix de Milo on stage, but by the time I take her back to the RV, she's just Payton.

Helping her into the loft, I follow her up and pull the curtain closed behind me. Never know when someone will be back. She bridges her hips to help me ease the elastic waistband over the curves of her hips and ass. She squirms as I kiss the insides of her thighs, until I bury my face between her legs. I feel her get instantly wet as I lick and suck around her labia. She moans and bounces while my tongue teases her clit. I feel her vagina throb and pulse, begging for my cock.

Unfastening my belt, I pull my pants down to my knees and slide easily inside of her slick pussy. She shoves her tongue in my mouth in return. To be honest, I haven't had sex since the last tour. I keep to myself at home. Not that there are many opportunities to meet people when you live in the middle of nowhere. Unless you're into tweakers.

Payton lubes her finger from her vagina and slips it into my ass. Given my four-months celibacy, this wasn't going to last long anyway, but now it's all over.

"It's okay, you can come in me," she moans. So I do. I collapse on top of her while I catch my breath, my heart racing. I roll over and she puts her head on my chest. We lay there in silence for several minutes, listening to each other breathe, when we hear the door creak open, followed by the unmistakable bull-in-a-china-shop sound of a band drunkenly returning from a party.

"Yoooooo! You in here?" Chris shouts.

"Yeah, man, be out in a minute." Not being in our twenties anymore, I don't have to worry about anyone being a drunken fool and trying to climb up here while Payton gets her clothes back on. Except Spiderweb. One never knows with him. She exits the loft first, greeted by the hoots and hollers you might expect from the band. She kisses my neck and ear as I open the door for her and she heads back to the party without another word.

"Damn, dude, nice one!"

"Uh, thanks? So you guys want to hit the road? Let's wake up in Oregon instead of waking up here and driving all day." I'm probably the most sober, so I offer to drive again. The most difficult part is the first few miles, navigating this beast through Sacramento's surface streets on our way back to Spiderweb's.

"Hey, brother, thanks for the good times. We'll see you on the way back. Leaving your key in the mailbox," I text, not expecting to hear back from him until at least the next day.

I crawl back to the kitchen area and ask Chris to line me up a couple rails while the other guys get our suitcases from Spiderweb's house. Gotta get my head straight for the next leg of the drive. At least, from here on out, we're taking the 5 and not the 99.

"Jess, you're oh-for-two, bro," I call into the intercom as I merge onto the freeway. They're done for the night. Lights click off and bunk curtains close. I tell Chris to pass me up the stash before he goes to bed and I settle in for a five-hour solo flight.

"You gotta try the water."

I finish telling the guys about some of the interesting features of this town as I sit down for a late breakfast, having caught a couple of hours sleep this morning after we rolled into the Creekside RV Park.

"What's up with the water?" Simon asks.

"Tastes different here. Just try it. There are drinking fountains all over town." The water tastes like rotten eggs. But I'm not going to tell them that, I'd rather they found out for themselves. Much funnier that way. I'm always looking for an opportunity to Roger Rabbit a situation.

Jesse is off renting us a van. It'll be easier to get around the next few days instead of trying to drive this thing through old downtown streets. We have a day off in Portland coming up and it would be cool to take the guys to some of my favorite spots around the city.

The white Kia Sedona races into the campground, throwing up dust in its wake. Brakes squeal as Jesse stops in front of the RV, hurtling the dust cloud in front of the minivan and directly at those of us gathered around the camp site.

I tell him to drop us at the bottom of the hill, by the bank of drinking fountains. Chris and Carlin hop out and go for a taste, immediately spitting it out and cursing me. I follow them onto the sidewalk, slapping my leg in mock laughter. The door to the van slides closed as Jesse pulls away. He and Simon volunteered to meet up with us after moving the gear to the venue. Jesse must be trying to make up for two days of slacking off.

"You guys wanna take a walk?" I ask, nodding up the hill. Carlin groans, but seems a little more receptive to the idea after Chris discreetly passes him a little glass vial.

"I'm thirsty. I need a drank!" I shout in my best Spiderweb impersonation.

As we crest the first hill, I weave off in the direction of an antique store. I always like searching for old stuff. It's all pretty interesting, from the music and books to the kitchen gadgets and clothes. My prize finds are old journals and collections of letters from people who are long-dead. They're becoming harder and harder to come by.

Chris, Carlin, and I spend a few minutes poking around in the old Happy Meal toys, vinyl records and comic books before Chris reminds me about that drink. We head single-file down the narrow, wooden catwalk to the stairs. As we're descending, I look in the bin below and spot the corner of a blue box with a red Galoob logo sticking out from underneath a ratty University of Oregon sweater.

It had to be before we moved to the mountains, I can remember the brown and orange carpet around the fireplace. Before my brother was old enough to walk. The house on the busy street by the freeway. I played for hours with this doll, expanding and retracting the arms and legs, swapping the propeller for the umbrella. One of my earliest memories is searching the house, inside and out, for my missing toy.

"One sec, I'm gonna get this." I carry the unopened box over to the counter where the hippie girl rings me up for the ten dollars shown on the little pink sticker. Her floor-length, tie-dyed skirt whips around as she gets a paper bag from the other side of the counter and unfolds it.

"Nice find. I was thinking about getting this for myself."

"Oh, sorry. You can totally have it."

"That's sweet," she grins, looking straight into my eyes. I can't tell where the brown part of her eyes end and the black part begins. "But I think you need it."

I look away.

"Hey, can I put one of these up in here?" Carlin asks, leaning between us with a poster for this evening's show.

"Too late," she says, pointing to the same flier, already hung in the front window. "Which one are you guys?"

"Right here," Carlin responds, pointing to our logo on the flier in his hands.

"Cool. I'll be there. I think the whole town will be. We haven't had much going on here lately."

"Same as everywhere," I say. "Just a broken, lonely civilization, looking for a connection anywhere we can find it."

"Exactly," she says, forcing eye contact with me again.

"Exactly!" Carlin echoes, causing her to look in his direction.

"Well, enjoy your doll." She deliberately touches my hand as she pushes the bag across the counter to me.

Next door, we find our place on a trio of torn vinyl barstools in the empty pub. "Something light and local, please," I nod to the bartender. It's funny, at home, I can't stand microbrews or the local fare. On the road, I try to eat and drink local as much as I can. Things do taste better on the road. For one, this beer doesn't taste like hops and goat piss.

"Same, but darker, brother," Carlin says, eyeing my beer. Chris holds up two fingers. I gag a little as I watch the chocolate porter slosh into the pint glasses like molasses. There's only one thing worse than IPA and that's any beverage that requires chewing. Beer shouldn't be thicker than a fruit smoothie. Remember Orbitz? Gross. But not nearly as disgusting as those aloe drinks with chunks of the plant. Barf. Oddly enough, boba is pretty good.

Carlin passes his glass back to the rail for a refill. "Make it three, mate," Simon says, sitting down next to Chris.

"Done already?"

"Yeah, man, they were all set up and had a whole crew to

help load in. Nice people up here."

"Hey, so I set up my congas. Hope that's cool, brotha," Jesse says across the three band members between us as he retrieves the beer Simon ordered for him.

"Sure, man. You know the songs?"

"More or less. I'll keep up." Some people are oblivious to my frustration at being presented as a 'jam' band. I'm all for improv and letting a song flow organically, within reason. Extended solos and what-have-you. At the very least, it makes sense that every band member know the song inside and out before deciding to fuck with it. But that's just me being anal. I need to just chill and let whatever happens, happen. With the exception of Simon, these cats would be all for the Grateful Dead approach to gigging. Minus the continuous touring. We don't play enough to be a good jam band.

"Let's finish these pints and head over for soundcheck. They asked us to be there by five." Three of us pull out our phones and check the time in perfect synchronicity. Tipping his head back, Carlin empties the remaining drops of brown liquid into his mouth and glances at the analog clock hung behind the bar. Four thirty-eight, bar-time.

In an attempt to maintain social distancing, the concert is being put on in the football stadium at the local college. It's cold as shit out on the field when we arrive. The grass crunches underfoot. I can't imagine anyone would want to come sit out here for three hours tonight. No different than a football game, I guess.

Whoever organized this show is a genius. Four stages on flatbeds, each set up with their own mixer and monitor system. The plan is, Simon tells us, they're just going to wheel each stage into position and hook it up to the house system when it's time to play. The stage platforms have curtains around them, allowing us to use them as a sort-of green room before we play. It'll help us not freeze to death before our set. Winter shows outdoors are the worst for playing guitar. It takes a full ten minutes of playing before my fingers start to work again.

No power on our platform. We watch as another act soundchecks from behind their curtain. Sounds good out here. We'll have to see how it sounds in the bleachers. When it's our turn, I fire up my amp and try to play some basic chords as my fingers defrost. This '66 Deluxe takes nearly as long to warm up as I do. I predict a rough first couple of songs.

An educated guess, really. And I'm right. We Cali boys aren't used to being able to see our breath on stage. Used to be, the stage lights would keep you warm, but now that everything's gone LED, we're left to keep ourselves warm by jumping around on our little pedestal. After a few rocky songs, we find our groove and let the cold power us through the next thirty-five minutes. The locals don't seem to mind the temperature, huddled together in small groups in the bleachers on either side of us.

As we finish our last song, they're unplugging the trailer and wheeling it to the locker rooms. No chance for an encore, they want to get the next act on without any intermission. The crew hauls our equipment down from the trailer and into the locker room, where they have beer and pizza waiting for us.

"Thanks, guys. Come back for a beer after the show," I say to the crew as they leave us to relax and defrost. The only place to relax, if you will, are the wooden benches laid out between the rows of lockers. As far as I can remember, I haven't had anything since the toast and eggs this morning. I'd better force down a couple slices of pizza.

I need to sit in a quiet place. It's getting hard to see on one side. I know what's coming next. I bite the inside of my cheek to distract myself.

"Yo, you dudes gotta come check this out," Carlin whispers, leaning out from between two rows of lockers. We grab our beers and follow him down a tiled corridor, past the showers.

"Hey, mind if we join you?" His voice reverbs across the

cavernous room as he throws open the double doors.

"For sure, guys, hop in." The band that was sound checking before us emerge as fuzzy silhouettes from the massive, steaming tubs. Simon says he'll meet us back at the RV and orders a ride on his phone. The rest of us strip down to our underpants and splash into the bubbling water. The hot water feels cold on my numb extremities.

"How was the set? To be honest, we couldn't hear much in our little tent out there."

"Pretty good, pretty good. It was nice to have all the monitors. We couldn't hear you either. How was yours?" The tattooed drummer, sitting next to me in the water, asks in return.

"Once my fingers unfroze, not so bad. It's been a while since I've done an outdoor show."

"Aren't you guys from California? We just figured you played outside year-round."

"That would be nice, but no. Maybe in LA or San Diego. Summer where we're from is face-melting hot and the winters aren't much warmer than this. We've got about four weeks a year with really nice outdoor weather."

He passes me a beer from the shelf behind him and gives us the low-down on the local scene in Oregon. I used to play up here a lot, but things sound like they've changed in the last decade. Way more competitiveness now, he says. The community isn't the same as it used to be. No camaraderie between bands.

"Yeah, sounds like everywhere I've been, actually. The same thing happened back home around ten years ago. I don't know what started it. A lot of venues closed, though."

"Hey bro, that girl from the store is here to see you," Chris calls to me from the doorway. She makes her way in, dressed the same as before, long hair flowing in harmony with her skirt. I start to get out of the tub to meet her, but she waves me back.

"Don't get up, I'll come to you." Dropping her bag on the ground and stepping out of her flip-flops, she climbs over the railing and into the water next to me, fully clothed.

"Hey."

"Hey." She makes intense eye contact with me again. It makes me feel safe and uncomfortable at the same time. "Zaya. We didn't get to officially meet before." She reaches a dripping arm from the water to shake my hand.

"Nice to *officially* meet you. Welcome to the after party."

"Thanks, but it's not a party yet." She stands, reaching for a bottle of wine from behind us. Wet clothes stick to her, revealing curves previously hidden by her loose-fitting skirt. The tattooed drummer notices her attempt and passes the bottle from the shelf. She pulls the cork and takes a long drink before settling in next to me and passing the bottle.

"I like your band. Very eclectic. Chaotic and organized." Finally a compliment I can agree with. I'm all over the place. My music is all over the place. The whole fucking world is all over the place and I'm not here to make sense of it. Someone finally noticed.

We finish the bottle and she says she wants to get out of here. Jesse's already drunk, but as the official tour manager, I let him know I'm going to bounce and to let me know when they want to leave. Putting dry pants over my wet underwear, I follow Zaya out to the parking lot.

"You're gonna freeze," I say, watching water pour from her skirt in a trail on the pavement behind her.

"It's okay, we're almost there." The lights flash on the yellow Volkswagen Beetle as we approach. She gets in the driver's seat and starts the engine, cranking the heat to max. Since the engine isn't warm yet, it blows cold air on my feet.

"There's something special about you."

"Thanks, there's something special about you, too." I've heard this before and I never know how to respond. I figure any time I can return the same compliment, that's the safest bet. Don't most people just say things for affirmation, anyway?

“No, I mean it. You sparkle.”

Peeling off her wet shirt, she climbs over the seat into my lap, leaning in for a kiss. I focus my energy on kissing her back with as much passion as I can muster. I think this is what passion is supposed to feel like. She reaches to the side and pulls the lever, leaning the seat back to its fully reclined position and slides to her knees on the floorboard in front of me. Unfastening my wet jeans and sliding them down around my ankles, she shoves my cock into her mouth. She makes out with it with the same fervor she kissed me with. Before long, she climbs on top of me, lifting her skirt and pulling her lace panties to one side, forcing me inside of her as she lowers her weight onto my lap.

Her dark nipples thrust out and read like braille under my tongue as I suck each one in turn. Leaning forward, she grabs my face and kisses me again. I reach up her neck and grab a handful of her hair at the scalp, squeezing gently. Her whole body shakes and quivers as she comes.

Breathing deeply into my neck, she takes a moment to recover. I can feel my pulse throbbing through my erect penis inside of her. She pushes herself up and off of me, climbing back to the floor to finish me off, smiling and beaming at me as she swallows.

After our clothes have dried, we dress and Zaya leads me, hand-in-hand down the main street, occasionally stopping to tell me about each of the local businesses and the people who work there. She’s lived here all her life. She says it’s hard watching the college students and tourists come and go every year. She says she might be ready for a change. I’m not sure what to make of that.

We’re sitting in the bar next to the antique store, the same one the band went to earlier, sharing a vodka-soda, when my phone vibrates.

“U@?”

I tell Carlin that I’m in town at the bar and I’ll meet them back at the school in fifteen. He responds and says they're leaving now and will pick me up. I apologize to Zaya and tell her that the road was calling. We exchange numbers and I give her our tour itinerary, hoping we can meet up in a few days when we're on our way home.

"What happened, bro, you look different," Chris says as I climb into the back seat of the van.

"I think he's in loooove," Jesse mocks.

"Yeah, she was a cool chick," I respond, monotone. "But we're on the road, so that's that."

Returning to the campground, we decide to stay the night and drive up in the morning. I probably could have had Zaya stay the night. Too late now. It's way earlier than we're used to being done with a gig, there's still time for a fire and some beers. We were smart enough to bring wood with us this time.

Jesse drags the ice chest out and dumps another twelve-pack on top. I reach down to the bottom for a cold one and raise my can to the group.

"Three days and nobody had to die. Congrats guys." They raise their beers in return and laugh. Jesse looks around like he's missing out on an inside joke. He's not wrong.

"Sorry, man. We swore we'd never speak of it again," I tease.

"Whatever, man. I don't want to know. Let's get fucked up."

"Fuck yeah!" Chris leaps to his feet. He and Jesse make their way inside and I can hear liquor bottles clang together. After waiting a couple minutes, I head into the rig, knowing they've got the coke lined up by now.

How predictable.

Just as we're crossing the bridge into Portland, the mist becomes a downpour. We're actually staying in Vancouver, so I follow the freeway across a couple more waterways to our exit and search for the Howard Johnson sign as I circle the mall. The parking lot is full of tree-trimmer and road-construction trucks, but eventually I find a place to park against the chain-link fence at the back of the overflow lot. We run for the front doors in a feeble attempt to stay dry. There's definitely an umbrella in the RV somewhere, I checked it off the list. But nobody bothers finding it.

Not expecting Jesse to be with us when I booked the tour, I only reserved two rooms. The hotel says they're full, so someone will have to sleep on a fold-out. I pass a pair of keys to Carlin and grab a couple of complimentary chocolate-chip cookies on my way to the elevator. Simon slips one of the cards from my hand as he joins me in the elevator. The rest of the band piles in and I tap the button for the third floor.

"I have a gig tonight. You should come," Simon says as the door to our room latches closed behind him.

"Yeah, dude, we all have a gig tonight. Don't worry, I'll be there."

"No, mate. After that." He tosses his phone on my bed. It's open to the profile of a local politician. He's known, even in California, for his rampant corruption and 'mismanagement' of funds. That should say something about this guy – being known in a state where literally every politician is a corrupt piece of trash.

"Okay, I'm down."

We take both the van and the RV down to the club, just in case. I've played this venue before. It used to be called something different. Something Saloon. The bar and the neighborhood are both a dive. I mean that in the nicest way possible. The whole area has a hip vibe to it. For Chinatown, as the municipally-installed signs proclaim, the architecture doesn't look Asian influenced.

Once we've lugged our gear across the street and into the empty venue, I order some plates of wings and nachos, hoping to entice Chris and Jesse to stay out of the strip club around the corner until *after* we play. Jesse's congas glimmer under the stage lights like a sweaty sheriff's deputy. He must have decided he's a permanent fixture in the band. Maybe I can convince Chris to say something to him. Or I can just let it go.

In the middle of my second guitar solo, Carlin slaps my shoulder with the back of his hand and nods to the door. Waiting for a wristband, in pleated, paisley skirt and olive-drab tank top, is Zaya. Is this stalker-status? How can she not be freezing? She makes her way toward the stage and I give her a wink over my teashade sunglasses to break her unwavering eye contact.

She's waiting for me around the side of the stage as we finish our set, but I only have time to acknowledge her from a distance before being shoved back up the steps for an encore.

"Hey, you should have told me you were coming," I say, making my way down from the stage a second time.

"Oh, sorry, is that okay?"

"Yeah, totally. I'm glad you did. I have to run an errand with our keyboard player real quick. You wanna take these guys over to the food trucks? You know where they are? I should be back in like an hour."

"Okay, sure. I know where they are."

"Just try to keep them out of the nudie bars," I say loud enough for the rest of the band to hear.

"Seriously, the fucking bald cap again?" The spirit gum

mats my hair as Simon brushes it around the edges of my scalp. The fake beard itches and I keep wanting to bite at the mustache as it tickles my lip. When I grow my annual beard, I'm constantly trimming my mustache with my teeth. This one tastes like dust and plastic.

"It's only for a few minutes."

"So what's the plan?" I ask, helping straighten his long, white beard as the glue gets tacky.

"For you, nothing. I just brought you along to watch. Try not to do too much, eh?"

I pull the cardigan sweater over my shoulders and climb out of the van, using the crook-neck cane Simon gave me for balance. I could have brought my own bamboo cane, had I known. I've had a lot of practice hobbling around with it these past few months. Since I got sick.

We finally have a break from the rain. We fall into character as we round the corner by the auditorium. A reverse Kaiser Soze.

"Target should be in the martini bar up the block."

We stop near the entrance of an anonymous concrete structure, hiding in the shadows of the neighboring multi-story office building. Simon looks intently up and down the street before proceeding.

Leaning against an aggregate-paneled trash can, Simon pulls a handkerchief out of his pocket and coughs violently into it, before shoving it back in his pocket and walking unstably over his cane to the other side of the street and back. I stand and watch as he repeats this act a few more times until the door to the bar opens and a quartet of fake-tanned men and women emerge, wearing overpriced suits, reeking of shopping mall colognes. These assholes who brag to their friends about their latest Italian shoes, Cuban cigars, French wines, while simultaneously telling the TV cameras how important it is to buy American. Hypocrites, the whole fucking lot of them.

Without warning, Simon drops his cane and falls to the

ground, not moving. I lean over him, trying to remain in character as I feign struggling to kneel next to him. One of the Italian-suit guys pushes me aside as he crouches next to Simon. The plastic in the pink Jackie-O suit pulls out her iPhone and the flash lights up.

"I'm gonna get you saving this guy's life for YouTube."

Simon opens his eyes and dry-heaves as his audience takes their front-row seats. They all tumble back in an attempt to dodge any vomit that may follow.

"I'm okay," Simon moans. He reaches both arms out and lets the two men lift him back to his feet. I pass him his cane and he leans over it feebly.

"You need an ambulance," one of the men tells him.

"No, no. It's okay. Happens sometimes. We'll just head home. Thanks for your help." Simon has dropped his accent and added some gravel to his voice. He gives me a light shove and I limp ahead of him towards the opulent granite building, covered in full-length window advertisements for the opera. We attempt to avoid stepping on any of the individuals spread out in stained sleeping bags on the sidewalk below these gaudy ads.

"So that's it? What happened?"

Simon tosses me a meth-baggie containing a half-dozen little red berries. "Abrin."

"Okay, but you didn't get them to eat these things." The little black device he shows me next looks like your typical novelty hand-buzzer. I reach for it and he pulls his hand away, shoving the plastic square into a baggie and into his pocket.

"Can't touch it, mate. Contaminated. I need to find somewhere to dump it," he says, peeling off his facial hair and shoving it into an old Albertsons bag between our seats. I pick around the edge of my scalp with my thumbnail to loosen the glue. He detours onto the bridge as we head back to the club and tosses the device over the edge, into the Willamette River. I take the opportunity to grab my jacket from the back seat and do the same with the body camera I've been carrying around with me.

To nobody's surprise, we find the rest of the gang back at the strip club, huddled around a four-top, paper takeout containers littered across the table. Zaya gets up and wraps her arms around me.

"Sorry, I tried," she shrugs. "I got you something."

Everyone gathers an armful of food and drink and we relocate to a vinyl booth against the back wall.

"Damn, darlin', you're the best," I tell Zaya, discovering injera and mesir wat inside the cardboard clamshell. She clings to me in the booth, watching me.

"Have you ever had it?"

"This is one of my favorites. How did you know?"

"I just listened to which restaurant was calling out to me. Are you a vegetarian?"

"Not all the time." I explain to her how I don't buy meat at home, but if it's prepared for me, I'll eat it. I tell her how I'm against factory farming, but the only thing worse than the systematic murder of millions of innocent animals is letting them rot in the trash.

Through the rhythm of the windshield wipers sweeping away the bulbous droplets, we watch Chris shiver impatiently in the queue, slowly snaking its way around the building. Zaya cuddles up against me on the bench seat in the back of the van, where we're seeing the least amount of action from the heater. I gave her my jacket, despite her claims that she was used to the weather.

Slamming the door, Chris passes the pink box around and we snack on Froot Loop and M&M-topped pastries as Simon takes us across the water and, before long, the border. We decide on a nightcap and I let Jesse know to lock up the rig and meet us out front for a ride to Red Robin.

The waitress admires my jacket on Zaya each time she comes by, eventually offering to buy it. It took me years of searching through thrift stores to find the Vietnam-era dress jacket with the appropriate stripes. It's not identical to John's jacket, but close. For one, this has airborne patches on it. Very few 'things' have sentimental value to me, but this might be one of them.

These guys eat non-stop. After the apps, the Ethiopian food, and donuts, I've more than met my quota for the day. There's still enough room for a beer or two. Carlin and Jesse order burgers and fries.

As things wind down, Simon leaves the keys on the table and announces it's past his bedtime. Zaya and I depart with him, her sharing his umbrella as we walk through the empty parking lots to our hotel.

The unwritten rule of every band I've ever been in is, if you're sharing a room and you want to fuck, just don't make a spectacle of yourselves...unless you're inviting the rest of the room to join. Zaya and I strip to our underwear and crawl under the blankets together. She puts my arm under her head and drapes her arm and leg across me. It's been a long time since I've shared a bed with someone. Six, eight months at least. For the first time in as many months, I actually sleep.

For once, I dream.

Not that I'm disappointed to realize it's Zaya kissing my neck and not my dogs as the sun peeks between the curtains and through my clenched eyelids. I do miss my pups, though.

"You were dreaming," she whispers.

"Yeah, weird. I never dream."

We tip-toe through the room and into the shower together, trying not to wake Simon. In musician-time, it's still early. In hotel-time, we need to check out in less than two hours.

"Let's go to the zoo today," Zaya says into my ear above the rhythm of the water splashing from our bodies onto the one-piece fiberglass shower stall. She turns around and asks me to wash her back before I can respond.

Before we make a final decision on where to go, I use the hotel phone to call over to the next room and wake up the guys. "Hello? Satan speaking. This is your wake-up call," I say into the receiver loud enough to disturb Simon. "You don't have to go home, but you can't stay here."

Downstairs, at the continental breakfast, the guys gorge themselves on pre-made pancakes, fluorescent-yellow scrambled eggs, and identical strips of bacon-like meat product. Zaya wants to meet her friends for brunch in Portland. It's kinda girlfriendy, but I did tell her we could hang out on our off-day. Looking at the greasy hotel food, sizzling under the heat lamps, I start looking forward to the restaurant.

Checking out, the hotel agrees to let us leave the RV in the back lot until we depart this evening. Two abreast in the three rows of the van, Jesse takes us to the southbound on-ramp. Before we've even made it back into Oregon, he jerks the wheel and swerves for the exit.

"Sorry, my bad. We have to stop. Chris and I were talking about this last night." He pulls in front of the massive warehouse building with its blue-and-yellow facade, letting us out at the curb. Carlin passes a joint around while we wait against the shopping carts for Jesse to find parking.

Inside, Chris and Jesse try out every piece of furniture in the winding corridors. I try not to let it get to me, focusing my attention instead on the beautiful woman who, for some inexplicable reason, is attached to my elbow right now.

"You coming to Seattle with us?"

"I wish. I have to be back at work tomorrow."

"Last thing we need is a Yoko Ono situation," Carlin jokes.

"Be nice, bro. Let's not forget that Yoko was the best thing to happen to John." Zaya smiles at me and blushes slightly, squeezing my arm.

Zaya's friends are waiting for us at a table in the vegan cafe when the van drops us at the corner. The young couple greets us warmly with hugs and cherry-lime mimosas, saying how perfect we are for each other. It's a little soon to tell, I think. From what I understand, they're not especially close. Old college friends who hang out when they're both in town. Zaya and this girl. Not the married couple, obviously.

Over my pecan chorizo, the girls ask me the standard interview questions. The kind of things I'd expect to be asked on an internet first-date. Zaya seems embarrassed, but I don't mind answering. Nothing to hide anyway. Her friends are asking for her benefit, anyway.

"What do you think of her art?" The one with the short haircut asks. Zaya stares straight ahead as I turn to look at her.

"Pardon?"

"Oh, sometimes she's shy." She goes on to explain that they were both art students in junior college. "You'll have to have her show you when you get back. Beautiful stuff."

"You're one to talk!" Zaya says, turning to show me some photos of trash-art on her friend's Instagram before changing the subject.

Walking south on 22nd Ave, we talk about the Victorian architecture, the graffiti, anything that catches our eye. It makes sense why so many people from Fresno move here. The neighborhoods aren't much different, but the weather and food are substantially improved. What I mean is, I like rain and vegan food. I'm less a fan of triple-digit summers and McDonalds.

A mile or so down the fragmented pavement, we reach our destination, the Lone Fir Cemetery. I don't know how this girl knows, but she definitely gets me. Pre-twentieth-century cemeteries fascinate me. I marvel at the statues and any headstone dating back to the era of the first settlers. I like to look up the interesting ones and see if there's a story. My attention is drawn to a row of matching stones, all bearing the same last name, the same date of death. Pulling out my phone, I search the names. Car accident. All of the family's children were in the vehicle. All are lined up here in front of me now, memorialized in granite for longer than most of them were alive.

We don't spend much time at the cemetery before Zaya calls a car to take us across the bridge to Washington Park. She wants to get some green tea before we visit the zoo.

"Ooh, I've always liked the literati ones," Zaya says as we stroll through the display of potted plants. "What about you?"

Stunned that she even knows the term 'literati', I pause. "I like the literati, too, but I seem to be partial to cascades in my own garden." I scroll through the photos on my phone, showing her my few remaining plants. A juniper, a manzanita, heavenly bamboo. The latter being pruned in the literati style.

"So what's this about your art?"

"Oh, it's nothing. I just like to paint sometimes."

"Well, let me see."

Retrieving her phone from her shoulder bag and passing

it to me, she swipes through several photos of mannequin torsos, painted in bold colors and patterns with hard lines. It reminds me of salvia art. Psychedelic, but not thoughtless. Somehow abstract and understandable at the same time.

"This is amazing. I need one for my studio. How much?"

"You can have one. Come by the shop on your way back to California." She leads me by the hand down the shoulder of the winding road, walking in the bike lane as cars whiz by behind us. I switch sides, letting her walk closer to the embankment. We pass a children's museum. I'd like to check it out, but don't say anything. Once, I went to a children's museum by myself. I enjoyed all of the hands-on exhibits, but being a childless adult man in a place like that was one of the most awkward and uncomfortable experiences of my life. Often, I would pull a notepad from my pocket and pretend to write to myself about the display in front of me, as if to validate my existence to the leering parents. Anyway, we're burning daylight.

This is my second visit to the Portland Zoo. It's one of my favorites. For a few years, I made the local zoos part of my routine when on the road. They come in all shapes and sizes. Concrete jungle to actual jungle. With few exceptions, I love all zoos. I know a lot of hardcore animal-rights people would disagree with me, but so long as the animals are cared for, the most important thing we can do to create compassion for animals is to educate future generations. Not to mention what they do for reproduction of threatened species. Portland, though, is unique in the experience it gives you, traveling from biome to biome.

Surrounded by burrowing arthropods and nocturnal mammals, Zaya pulls my elbow, drawing me in for a kiss, before we exit the corridor into the daylight. It feels early, but it will be dark soon. And cold. Passing the tigers, into the African savanna, she tells me, "Did you know a rhino's horn is made of hair?"

I did know this, actually. Keratin. Following the curve of the path, we share other random trivia. I tell her a koala has near-identical fingerprints as humans, but a smooth brain. She says a Hyacinth macaw has a stronger bite than a shark.

"I've always wanted a hyacinth," I say. Yeah, they *can* bite that hard, but I wouldn't need to give them reason to.

It's starting to sprinkle. The sky could open at any moment, so I page a ride and we finish the loop, stopping by the gift shop before we exit.

Running through the rain, away from the car, we shake the water from our hair before I open one side of the double door for her to enter the bookstore ahead of me.

Powell's is a mandatory stop every time I visit the area. They have everything here. Just to prove it, I ask the cashier where I can find books on seventeenth-century Japan. She directs me upstairs, where I find an entire shelf on the subject. Zaya and I have separated. I'm not going to go looking for her right now. We'll run into each other eventually. After we've each browsed the subjects that are of particular interest to each of us.

I find a few cheap, used books. I can't pass up discount nonfiction. A yoga book, something on the 1906 earthquake, a home-repair handbook. I guess a lot of this stuff is irrelevant now, with all of my home improvement and fitness questions answered by the internet. With video. I still like the feel of paper books. I refuse to own a Kindle.

On my way back down the stairs, I pass Carlin and Simon, heading the other direction.

"Hey, what up? What have you guys been doing today?"

"Well, this guy bought a hurdy-gurdy," Carlin says, pointing his thumb at Simon.

"Nice! I've never played one of those before."

"Me neither," Simon responds, leaning against the railing to let a group pass by.

"Look what I found," Zaya says, coming around the corner at the top of the stairs. She's holding up a familiar slate-gray cover, congested with hand-written notes, marred by a blood-stained logo taking up too much space on the front.

"Yeah, I don't recommend that one. Zero stars."

"Too bad, I'm buying it. You're famous!"

I published the three-hundred-ish page collection of my personal essays in the hopes that it might help people understand mental health better. That we're more than just a diagnosis. Or, in most cases, a misdiagnosis. It's some of the more interesting, albeit convoluted writing I've ever done. Nevertheless, I'm not a fan of people I know reading it. Too much vulnerability. Too much darkness. I unpublished it within a year of release, but there are obviously a few copies still floating around.

Meeting the rest of the crew outside, I suggest we check out the underground tunnels, but they're set on going for dinner. Maybe next time, I tell myself again – the same as every time I visit. At least they're not just sitting in the hotel room, eating takeout. I'll have to plan a trip to come back to visit Zaya and we can do some exploring.

The Caribbean restaurant we decide on is just down the street from where Simon and I took our walk last night. Carlin gives his spare change to a shabbily-dressed man, leaning against the wall. He's asked for change six more times before we make it to our table. The rest of us do our best not to disrupt the inhabitants as we zig-zag our way down the sidewalk.

As we've known all day, Zaya and I eventually have to say goodbye. She kisses me in the rain outside of the restaurant for longer than I'm used to a kiss lasting before climbing into the green Focus, waiting to take her to her friends' house.

Jesse drops us back at the hotel to retrieve the RV and heads out of the parking lot and onto the main road to drop the rental off. We get the heat started while we wait. Chris crushes a few white stones into a chalky powder, offering me first choice. I pull the coiled bill from my pocket and twist it between my fingers to tighten it into a stiff rod (heh) and lean over the table.

Our rooms aren't ready.

We're several hours early for check-in. It's not even check-out time for the other guests yet. Everyone's tired from staying up during the drive, drinking, smoking, trying to make out Mount Rainier in the darkness. They said they'll try to have some rooms for us in an hour. We decide to wait at the Denny's across the street.

"This is one of the areas Gary Ridgway used to hang out," I tell the guys as we sit down.

"Who?" Chris asks.

"The Green River Killer. Used to cruise up and down this very street, looking for victims."

"What about Dahmer, wasn't that around here?"

"I think you mean Ted Bundy. Yeah, in this area, but not right here. Dahmer was in Minnesota."

Denny's isn't exactly one of my *least* favorite restaurants. As far as short-order goes, it's better than IHOP or the other one. I mean, it is what it is, but on the road, I always prefer something more interesting. I played in too many bands who ate Denny's and drive-thru exclusively on the road, so when I do it now, I feel like I'm committing some kind of sin. Why eat the same thing on the road that we can eat at home? Either way, I'm starving. I devour the entirety of my Lumberjack Slam before finishing leftover pieces of toast and sausage from around the table. I think sausage is the grossest of the breakfast meats, but I'm not going to let those poor animals go to waste.

"Damn, dude."

"I know. Now all I need is access to our rooms before the food coma sets in."

We wait out the clock for a full hour before returning to

the hotel lobby. Our rooms are ready. Both suites.

"Good morning! How did you sleep?" Zaya texts.

"Lol. I haven't yet," I respond before passing out on the couch. I don't even bother to pull the mattress out. Jesse and Chris can have the beds. I'm so exhausted, I could sleep on the floor at this point.

It's hot in the room and I sleep restlessly for only a couple of hours before groggily staggering to the shower to clean up for tonight's gig. Zaya's sent me a few more messages, photos of her mannequins, asking me to choose one. I ask her if I can wait until I see them in person.

The venue is a long, narrow theater with an open ground floor and seating upstairs. Barely thirty feet separate the front of the stage from the opposite wall.

Finishing with an early sound-check, we hike the steep driveway back to the street and into the adjoining brewery. I'm relieved to see a vast selection on tap outside of the standard IPAs. Carlin and I find a high-top table in the corner, leaving the rest of the band at the bar. He wants to figure out the game-plan for tomorrow night. His research isn't nearly as meticulous as Simon's, but he has enough information for us to get where we need to go. I question whether we should involve Simon in this venture. At this point, and as far as I can tell, he and Carlin are oblivious to the activities of the other. I'd probably better leave it that way. Without discussing too many details, we decide to head straight to the hospital after our set. The hard part will be coming up with a believable excuse.

The thin strip of stage is backed by a curtain and a six-foot drop. The drum riser, barely four-feet square, leaves Chris dangling precariously over the back of the stage as we play. I stay close whenever possible, never knowing when I might have to reach out and grab him.

During our encore, Satchel runs down the stairs and grabs a spare microphone, singing along with Crystal Blue. I used to sneak nips from a flask with this guy behind random clubs over a decade ago. I didn't even know he was here tonight. Finishing our closing number, I segue into Girl From Oklahoma, Carlin passes his guitar off to our guest. He plays leads on the acoustic over my electric rhythm. We trade licks for a few phrases at the end before ducking off the side of the stage and behind Chris' riser.

"Right on, brother! Good to see you again," I say as we hide in an alcove down the corridor from the gathering crowd "What are you even doing up here?"

"Just visiting some old friends. I had no idea you were playing again."

"Yeah, as much as I can. I'm getting too old for this shit." We both laugh, making our way out the back door for a cigarette while waiting for the band to load the gear. I'll let them handle my load-out tonight. They'll understand. Anyway, that should be Jesse's job. I've given up on keeping him off the stage during our sets.

Satchel and I say our goodbyes. I invite him to party with us, but he says he can't tonight. Flying back to Cali tomorrow. "Keep in touch, bro. It's been too long."

In the morning, we visit Pike's to check out the juggling fishmongers and drink Starbucks. That's not the same as Denny's because I don't drink Starbucks at home. I don't eat at Denny's either. Whatever. Pike's is campy and touristy, but we enjoy it anyway. I'll take touristy over drive-thru any day. I get some falafel, since it's not something I'm likely to run across again on our trip. Usually, I'm not a breakfast person. That is, I don't eat in the morning. I like breakfast foods just fine. Not that falafel is a typical breakfast food.

After throwing a few bills in the guitar case of a one-man-band in exchange for letting us watch him for a few minutes, we return to the parking garage and navigate our oversized vehicle through the merciless Seattle streets and back to the freeway.

The snowbanks grow exponentially the further inland

we go. Jesse is white-knuckled, squinting to make out the road between swipes of the windshield wipers. I tell him to pull over and we get out, fastening our coats, into the slush. Lining the chains up with each tire, I call to Chris to pull the rig a few feet forward. He overshoots the mark and has to back up slightly so we can fasten the clasps. Back on the road, it doesn't feel like it's handling any differently.

I should take the opportunity to check messages and handle some business. No bars. We're outside of the service area. I open the fridge and pass out a round of cans.

"You want one up there?"

"Fuck, man, I better. I need to relax."

Chris reaches into the cockpit and pours a beer into Jesse's Starbucks cup. I dump a couple of Ativan from the bottle on the counter, swallowing one with a long pull from my beer and passing the other up to the front.

The other four of us settling in around the table, I pull out a stack of 80's and 90's Trivial Pursuit cards and quiz the guys on the music and movie categories while we pass around a preroll from the dispensary in Seattle. They'd probably be pretty good at the sports category, too, but I don't know shit about sports, so I skip that section of the card. This is going to be a long drive. It's not incredibly far. Only halfway across the smallerish state. But at this point, with the visibility and road conditions, we can't go any faster than about thirty miles-per-hour.

The brain hole starts again and I need to get horizontal. Sliding from the booth to the couch, I lay down and close my eyes, still answering trivia questions as they're read aloud. It's hard to focus on any conversation beyond the immediate question and answer. I'm too nervous about the drive to sleep. Even in good weather, I would have a hard time.

Not having brought along any kind of galoshes, my feet are soaked by the time we get our gear loaded into the venue. I can tell the guys are disappointed with the size of the venue.

"Hey, don't worry. Remember last time? We thought it was going to be a shitty room and it turned out pretty cool. We're still getting paid either way."

There's no stage. No PA. The manager asks us to set up in the back corner, where they have a roll-out projector screen. More bare floors. Reverb city. I appreciate the owners of these small bars and restaurants trying to keep independent music alive, I really do, but it only takes a few hundred dollars to make a venue sound good. Tolerable, at least.

The crowd is small, but supportive. Especially for a Thursday in February. We're opening for a local cover band. Towards the end of our set, the bar starts to fill in. Not unusual in a town like this. It's not glamorous, but everyone seems to dig it.

Carlin and I can't get out of there fast enough once our set is over. He calls an uber and has the driver drop us at the entrance to the local emergency room.

We go through the double doors and wait a moment for the car to leave. Back outside, in the snow, we hide around the concrete wall near the ambulance entrance. Then, shivering, decide to relocate to the old wooden bench, where we can see the door, each lighting a cigarette as we sit. Ten-fifteen. According to Carlin's notes, Lydia should be leaving soon. Presumably, through this door, as it's closest to the employee parking lot. Had we involved Simon, we probably could've got the info on her car, but I doubt he'd approve of our little excursion.

"Sure you're ready for this?" I ask.

"Yeah, man. Gotta do the right thing for those kids."

Carlin lights another cigarette, offering me one from his pack. I wave in the negative. It's too much for me to chain-smoke them like that. Before he finishes, we see a short, middle-aged woman with long, black hair leave through the security door. Looks like our target, based on the photos. She walks past us, unaware, the blue light of her phone illuminating her face as she crosses the driveway without checking for traffic.

Carlin gets up from the bench and follows several paces behind her. I'm close pursuit. More than anything, I'm here for moral support. And to help if he gets into trouble.

"Hey, Lydia!" He yells just as she gets to her car at the far end of the darkened lot. She turns to look at the voice, squinting against the distant halogen lighting. Clearly, she's still trying to figure out who is calling to her as Carlin slams her against the side of the Silver Lexus SUV. He's on top of her before she even hits the ground. Pulling her by her hair, he smashes the back of her head into the asphalt once and she falls limp.

Her keys lie on the blacktop a few feet away. Carlin reaches for them and hits the button to open the rear hatch. I grab her feet and help him load her into the back. He climbs into the driver's seat and starts the engine. After pressing the button and waiting an eternity for the back hatch to close, I make my way to the passenger door.

"You know where you're going?"

"Yeah, I got it."

Several turns later, we pass through an underpass and onto a frontage road that eventually branches away from the freeway, turning from pavement to dirt as it heads toward the river.

Carlin stops the vehicle a couple hundred yards from the end of the road and switches off the lights. Waiting for a moment to make sure nobody is around, he hops out, leaving his door open and circles around to the back of the SUV, pressing up on the hatch in an attempt to force it to open faster.

She's conscious, but not alert. Clearly unaware of what's happening. Carlin lifts her over his shoulder and carries her up to the empty seat. From the passenger side, I help him get her buckled in and situated, as if she were driving. He rolls down the window and gently closes her door. Reaching through, he shifts into drive. Using the steering wheel to aim the Lexus at the dead-end sign overlooking the river, he walks alongside the SUV as it creeps along.

I stand next to a dirt pile, watching from the edge of the path. Thirty or so feet from the end of the road, Carlin runs out at an angle and away from the rolling vehicle.

With a crash, the front bumper topples the aluminum sign, sending it into the ravine just ahead of Lydia's car. We walk casually to the edge and watch as the vehicle sinks, the icy water pouring through the open window. Waiting several minutes to ensure she doesn't swim to the surface, we start our trek back, passing under the freeway. There's a bank of commercial buildings ahead, so we decide to stop there to find some shelter from the cold.

All closed. They're some kind of warehouses or something. No cars in the lots, the lights are off. Carlin pulls out his phone and orders a car. Fortunately, we only have to stand at the edge of the knee-deep snow for a couple of minutes before our ride pulls up. It's the same blue Hyundai from before. Fuck.

"Whoa, how'd you guys get way out here? I thought you were going to the hospital?" Double Fuck.

Thinking on his feet, Carlin responds, "Yeah, we were. Our friend was supposed to be there, but he wasn't, so we've been going around town, looking for him. Tall, long hair, green sweatshirt?"

"Huh. Nope, haven't seen anyone like that." Our driver flips around in the deserted parking lot and orients back toward the bar. "Where you guys from?"

"Rockford, by way of Fresno." Goddammit, Carlin. What the fuck, dude?

They make small talk, mostly about the weather differences between Washington and Illinois. He's making too much of an impression on this driver. If the cops start asking around, he might remember picking us up in the middle of the night, not far from the river. I don't want to stress Carlin out, so I let it slide. We're not connected to this lady. We have no known motive. Aside from the gig, there's no record we were even in Yakima. Well, the cab rides. Now I understand why Simon is always renting a car.

Carlin asks to be dropped off a couple blocks from the venue, in front of a liquor store. Inside, he grabs a few bottles of name-brand vodka and whiskey, not seeming to care which he chooses. We trudge our way through the layers of salt and melting snow on the sidewalk, it's just one intersection before we're in front of the bar, where Chris is huddled in front of the door, smoking a cigarette with great urgency.

"What? Where'd you guys go? We were looking for you."

"Irish exit. You know how we do." Carlin holds up the plastic bags from the liquor store. "Supply run."

"We loaded your gear. You're welcome. Everyone is ready to get the hell out of here."

Without bothering to go through the venue, we circle around to the back, where the RV is waiting, idling. Simon tosses an envelope at me when I come through the door.

"Thanks for telling us where you went, mate." He's one to talk. I can't tell if he's eyeing me suspiciously or teasing. Tearing off the end of the envelope, I pass hundred-dollar bills around the room, rolling mine into a tight tube as I slide into the booth next to Jesse, across from Chris.

"You guys call it tonight. Want to stay here or try to make it out through the storm? Who's fucked up?"

They all want to leave tonight. Even with the heater on, we're freezing in here. Simon, Jesse, and I agree to take an hour at the wheel each. It's a solid six-hour drive to the next gig. Our longest of the trip, I'd say. If we can make it to Portland, the roads should be clear enough for an easy drive the rest of the way. That, or we'll find somewhere to park and wait out the storm. I'm feeling particularly relaxed about this drive.

The rain breaks as the sun comes up.

Just as we're pulling into Eugene, the sunrise peaks through the clouds and reflects off the slick road in front of us. From the front seat, I direct Simon to our motel, a retro-looking, single-story number with green doors facing the parking lot. The rooms are standard for a roadside motel. Grimy, commercial-grade carpet, plasticky bedspread, an out-of-place table with two chairs next to the window. The faint smell of mold peeking out from under the more overwhelming odor of cleaning products. Better than nothing. At least it's cheap.

My phone vibrates in my pocket. It's Zaya. I step out onto the concrete walkway, leaning against the wrought-iron railing and swipe the green circle. She says she just wanted to hear my voice. She missed me.

Do I miss her, too? The companionship is nice, but I don't think I caught feelings quite so quick, like she did. She's asking me how our trip to Washington went. Did we have any excitement?

"Not at all, it's actually been a really quiet trip." I tell her about playing with Satchel. She's never heard of him. I'm not surprised. But she seems pleased that I had a good time.

"I've been reading your book," she says. I gulp. Here it comes. "You're really brave to put all that out into the world. I don't think most people would do it. I wouldn't."

"Thanks," I say, a little confused. I'd expect anyone who catches a glimpse into my darkness to make a run for it. That's what they've always done in the past.

"I'm sorry you had to go through all of those things. I guess that's what it took to make you who you are today." I don't feel like I'm anything special today, just like I didn't feel like I was anything special ten years ago.

She has to get to work and I'm freezing out here, so we end our call, promising to talk later that evening. Back inside, I catch a couple hours of sleep before waking the band and directing them back outside so we can get to load-in.

"This is more like it," Carlin says, pulling a drum case through the back door of the club. Big stage, lots of lights, the opposite of last night. Our set is sandwiched between two local bands. I looked them up, much harder sound than we're used to. We can only hope their fans don't chase us off the stage.

"I can't pay you a full band-wage every night, y'know," I tell Jesse as he brings his congas up the steps.

"It's cool, brother. It's more fun to play than to watch." He sets up his stands off to the side, near Chris' drums. It's a spacious stage, but they have all three bands backlined up here. Six amps, three drum kits, eleven dudes. Not much room to move around. When it's time for us to go on, at least some of this will be out of the way.

Leaning against the bar, we sip beer from clear plastic cups and listen to the opening band as they do their sound check. They. Are. Loud. It won't be so bad with a room full of people, but right now, I can barely stand it. The toneless blare of the mid-scooped Marshall stack fighting to drown out the machine-gun sound of a double-kick pedal.

"Sorry, I gotta wait outside," I shout over the noise in the general direction of our group.

The guys follow me out to the parking lot, having already finished our sound check, and we walk as a pack down the sidewalk, looking for something local to lay a base-coat down with.

A block south of the venue, there's a towering Victorian mansion that's been converted to a restaurant. The menu-board in front looks decent enough, so we give it a shot. Inside, glass shelves rise to the ceiling behind the polished oak bar, advertising every flavor of liquor one could imagine. I order a house special, a fruity cocktail. It's out of character for me, but I notice it's nearly the same as the signature cocktail I served when I was bartending, except mine had blue curacao instead of melon liqueur. And no cream.

I don't care for it. Too sweet and too many flavors. I didn't care much for my own cocktail, either, but I didn't make it for me. The girls at the bar seemed to enjoy it. Chris, Carlin, and Jesse have each ordered a fishbowl cocktail. The menu says it's meant to serve four people, but it doesn't say anything about how many musicians it's meant to serve. I don't know where the hell Simon went.

The veggie panini is meh, but at least it'll give me something to put a gallon of beer on top of. This place seems to be trying to specialize in crepes, in addition to the otherwise random menu of burgers, pasta and salad. I could get down on some crepes, but not if I'm going to spend the rest of the evening drinking. Not if I want to keep them down. That doesn't stop Chris and Jesse from ordering several plates of crepes and washing them down with a fishbowl of clear-blue liquor.

It's always been natural for me to compartmentalize. Ignorance is bliss. Years of drinking to block out the bad stuff. It always comes back. Carlin, on the other hand, has his phone out, reading news articles about the Lexus SUV found in the Naches River. One decedent. No signs of foul play. They suspect she took a wrong turn and couldn't see the end of the road in the snow. Happens all the time.

"Stressful trip for you," I say, leaning over his shoulder and reading the article.

"Yeah, no, I'm fine."

There's a staggered line waiting to get into the venue. Groups of college students, mostly, crammed together under the eaves and overhangs of nearby businesses, attempting to stay dry. The bouncer stops us at the door, directing us to the back of the line, several hundred yards down the block. As a group, we pull up the sleeves of our jackets, showing the wristbands they gave us with our drink tickets when we got here the first time. He apologizes and opens the door, letting us into the cold, vacant hall. The rat-a-tat of the kick drum and bass guitar echo through the hallway. I wait for the opening band to finish their warm-up before letting myself into the empty auditorium and making a beeline for the bar, drink ticket in hand. Has the band been jamming the whole time we were at dinner? If so, I feel bad for the staff. The night hasn't even started yet and their hearing must already be wrecked.

The single green room is crowded with members of all three bands. Nowhere to sit. Guitar and bass players tune strings while drummers diddle and paradiddle away on practice pads or pillows.

"Shit, if I knew all this beer was back here, I wouldn't have gone to the bar!"

"Help yourself, bro. I'm Darren." I shake the moisture of the ice chest from my hand, wipe it on my jeans and shake his hand. "Welcome to Oregon."

"Thanks, brother. Actually, we were just here a few days ago. On our way home, now." He plunks at his guitar, turning the silver key on the headstock, then starts running scales at ludicrous-speed. Finding a seat on the counter, I watch him climb up and down the fretboard, finishing my beer at the pace he's keeping on the guitar.

"Nice chops, dude. I can't play like that. Double-tapping is a stretch." He laughs and leans the guitar against the couch, it's pointy cutaways sliding across the linoleum floor until it finds its equilibrium. Darren takes me around the room, introducing me to the rest of his band-mates, as well as the guys from the noisy band, who are getting ready to head back to the stage already. We can hear the voices, the shuffling bodies, coming from outside the door, which has been left ajar to air out the stink and carbon dioxide of mid-grade weed and a dozen sweaty musicians.

"We were listening to your album at rehearsal last week," Darren's drummer says as we clink our beer bottles together in introduction. "Good shit, man. Good shit. Is that just you guys?"

"For the most part, it's just three of us. Carlin sings, Chris does percussion and I do everything else. Jesse, Simon, and a few other friends made guest appearances."

"Shit, and you're worried about double-tapping?" Darren says to me, gregariously socking me on the shoulder.

The opening act starts their set and our conversations grind to a halt. Most of us crowd outside and against the back door, under a few shared umbrellas. We pass around joints and smoke copious amounts of cigarettes while waiting for the first band to finish their set. Grey-white clouds hang under each umbrella. In turn, we each go inside for a few minutes to show our support to the band. Even if we don't really dig their sound, it's what we do. When we hear them announce their last song, the lot of us line the back hallway and congratulate the departing act on their set, while helping them over extension cords and down the stairs with their gear.

Shoving a few beers under our arms and grabbing our instruments, the five of us file onto the stage to find our places for the next hour. We're way too loud, in my opinion. There's no need for our band to be at the volume of the metal band before us. I keep turning down my amp, but the sound guy keeps turning me up in the mains. In the monitors, too. I can't see more than a shadow behind the soundboard, through the stage lights, but hoping I have his attention, I point at my guitar, then my ear, then point straight down. He catches on and dumps my guitar from the monitor. It's still hella loud out on the floor, I'm sure, but the rest of the band will appreciate not being blasted out by my guitar for an entire set. Between songs, I twist my amp so it's pointing at the band, now that they don't have a monitor mix. Simon gives me a thumbs-up from across the stage without looking over. I can't hear myself now, but I know my parts.

Two or three songs from the end of our list, we go into Power Over. Like every other song we've played tonight, the audience bobs around. Or hops. Or whatever version of dancing it is people do to alternative-rock music. As Carlin gets into the second verse, a mosh pit breaks out and quickly deteriorates into a full-blown fight. We finish the song, but by that time beer bottles and other debris are flying across the room, some of it at the stage. Unplugging, we run off stage and into the corridor. Chris' crash cymbal rings as a beer bottle shatters across it. Our new friends are waiting in the hall, telling us how badass that was. They try to get a crowd wound up like that and we do it without even trying. Darren says he's jealous.

Certain the cops will be here any minute, we're ready to abandon our show and hide backstage until the room clears. The other bands won't hear of it. They insist we get back on stage and finish our set, pushing us back up the steps. The neck of my Strat bangs against the handrail as I stumble back up to the stage. Shit. I try to tune it before Chris clicks off the next song, Rockstar Nobody. Fortunately for me, he has to clear broken glass from his snare before he can sit down. I wonder how this audience is going to react to us closing with Crystal Blue. I laugh to myself at the mental image of people moshing to a hippie anthem as I finish my solo.

We're barely off the stage when Darren and his crew are plugging in and starting their first song. They want to keep the angry energy of the crowd going. Crystal Blue didn't help mellow people out. It wouldn't. We played it harder and angrier than we ever have.

Several musicians crowd into the RV with us after the set, drinking vodka from the bottle, crushing piles of cocaine across the counters and, eventually, giving Jesse directions to Darren's house. It's not far. Walking distance from our motel in nicer weather.

He meets us in his front yard with beers and invites us inside. Random concert-goers are starting to trickle in. This must be the official after-party destination. The two-bedroom Craftsman fills quickly and before long, I'm uncomfortable and claustrophobic.

My phone buzzes, showing Zaya's name and number on the screen. Outside, I answer and try to find a quiet place on the covered porch to talk. Turns out I'm not on the phone long. She's in town, having missed our set, and is wondering where to find us. Within a few minutes, she's getting out of a car and wrapping her arms around me on the porch. Still not wearing a jacket. I don't know how she can handle it. I can see my breath.

"Did you miss me?" She asks.

"You know it," I say, leading her into the house for a drink. We can't find a comfortable place to stand, so we take our beers out to the rig for some privacy. She leans against me on the couch, putting her feet up across the armrest.

"What do you think about me going back with you?"

"Yeah, for sure. We'll give you a ride home tomorrow."

"No, I mean going back with *you*." She pokes at my thigh. Uhhh. I don't know how to respond to this request. Is it even a request? Sounds like she's pretty certain of herself. I don't answer for a long time.

"Well, think about it."

We pull the blinds apart to look at the commotion outside. Several young men have evacuated the house, pushing, shoving, and throwing punches at each other. Judging by what we can hear breaking, it's happening inside, too.

Chris and Carlin run down the concrete steps, dodging flailing arms and legs on their way back to the RV. I throw open the door and lock it behind them. Simon is next, turning wildly away from the bodies and glass bottles flying at him.

"Where's Jesse?" We all ask as Simon climbs on board. He shrugs. Several others try to open the door to get in as the wail of the sirens gets closer. The band members I recognize from the green room, I let in, ignoring those who look like they're participating in the action. Bodies scatter from the front yard in every direction as red and blue lights come around the corner and race towards us. From the middle of it all, Jesse comes running for the RV, holding his pants up with one hand, eyebrow bloody and swollen. He climbs on and I latch the door behind him. Of course he would be participating.

"Let's go!" Someone calls from the kitchen area.

"You want to drunk-drive an RV full of drugs out of here when we're surrounded by cops?!" I shout back. "Everyone be quiet. We'll just wait it out." I flip the cabin lights to night mode and everyone settles into a seat or bunk, sipping their drinks quietly and not speaking as we wait, peeking through the blinds. Six or eight police officers stand in Darren's yard, chatting amongst themselves and generally avoiding work for what must be an hour. A sergeant pulls up in front of his house and rolls the window of his cruiser down. Immediately, the officers scatter and head for their own cars. Ha. Lazy bastards.

Finally, we're clear to go. Unloading our extra passengers, we thank Darren for the interesting evening and fire up the engine. It's a two-minute drive to the hotel and the end of another successful-ish night on the road. Zaya and I opt to stay in the RV and give the rooms to everyone else.

She climbs on top of me in the loft, undressing us both in the process. Maybe I do want her to come back with us.

We're racing a blizzard.

Heading south, as soon as we reach the mountains, the storm moves in behind us. It's in the rearview mirror, getting closer each time we stop. In Ashland, we pick up Zaya's luggage and some of her mannequins.

"Whoa, that's sweet! Did you make these?" Carlin asks as he loads the painted torsos into the compartment under the rig. Zaya nods, passing him her suitcase. She smiles sheepishly, not showing her teeth. Normally she is wearing a wide, toothy smile.

We wait impatiently for the gas tank to fill, watching the dark clouds moving in from the north, then for Chris to return from taking a shit in the gas station. He hurries back, arms piled high with energy drinks.

We make it over the hill and to a lower elevation before the storm reaches us, slipping and sliding across both lanes of the highway in the process. After the second time losing his pan of eggs from the stove, Chris opens a box of granola bars and stumbles uneasily to the table, where the rest of us are holding on for dear life. More than once, I was certain we were going to go over the edge or into a snowbank.

We decide to stop in Weed for lunch. Mostly because the guys think a town named 'Weed' is funny.

"Look, there's a place called Black Butt, too," Chris says, pointing out the window.

"That's Butte," I correct him.

The jalapeno ale pairs nicely with the giant soft-pretzel in front of me. The weather is nice outside, considering. Still pretty cold. But clear and crisp. We sit together around the picnic table, crunching our feet in the slush below as we marvel at the white mountain beside us.

"I'm climbing that thing some day."

"Wait, what mountain is that?" Chris asks.

"Shasta. I've always wanted to hike an active volcano."

Jesse looks from the mountain to me and back again, setting his pizza on the ranch-covered plastic plate. "Hold on. You're telling me that it could erupt at any time and we're just gonna sit here and have lunch?"

"Well, yeah. It could, I guess. But they built whole cities around it, so I think we're safe."

"You're crazy if you want to hike that," Carlin adds.

"I'll go," Zaya says, still not wearing a jacket.

With the weather and additional stops, we're almost late for load-in. The promoter and engineer meet us outside to give the rundown on the stage setup and format for tonight's show. One of the other bands has offered to share their drums and amps. Chris and I peek through the backdoor to check out the gear they have on stage. We agree to use the backline and grab our gig bags from the RV loft. It's a pain in the ass to load them in and out of the overhead area multiple times per day, but safer than sticking them down below to slide around with several hundred pounds of amps, trap cases, and PA speakers.

Our band is hard to fit into a single genre. Is it alternative rock? Hard blues? Hip-hop and funk? It doesn't matter to us, we've never tried to fit into a mold, even though we know it's smarter from a marketing standpoint. The goal never was to get famous. But since we're so all-over-the-place, we get paired with every kind of act you can imagine. Last night was heavy metal – 'nu-metal', I guess. I've always hated that term. Tonight we're playing with a couple of punk bands, not unlike the group from Albuquerque. I've never heard of them, but I guess they're hot-shit right now. Chris knows about them. Psychedelic, country, burlesque, we'll play with them all. They're the ones doing us the favor, inviting an out-of-genre band to their shows.

Excused from load-in and sound check, we explore the halls of the old theater. It's like most of the mid-century, art-deco theatres back home. Abstract-patterned casino carpet. Extravagantly carved ceilings and columns. Murals. Sconces and chandeliers. Seating for several hundred with no dance floor. Pop-up bar with two choices of beer or wine. Not that it should be different, we're only a few hundred miles from home.

Carlin and Jesse lean over the counter of the snack bar. "Nobody here," Carlin calls to us over his shoulder.

"Should we just help ourselves?"

"That probably wouldn't be cool. We have beer in the rig."

On our way back to the parking lot, the promoter, Monica, stops us in the aisle to let us know our dressing room is ready. *Our* dressing room? I expected to just use the RV as our green room. We added this stop last minute, so I wouldn't blame them for not planning for us. It should have been the first show I booked. Touring is all about the weekend gigs.

Backstage, in the literally-green room, we find trays of cured meats, aged cheeses, cocaine, Humboldt weed, cupcakes, veggies, mini-bottles of liquor.

"Hey, thanks, Monica. Much appreciated. Where's the other band?"

"Through the door, if you want to open it. You each have your own rooms."

Chris and Jesse want to go warm up on the backline before doors open. Zaya follows, looking for the restroom. Three dressing rooms backstage and only one bathroom, occupied. I stop Carlin from opening the door to our neighbors, passing him a plain-white envelope, my home address hand-written in neat block-lettering on the front.

"What's this?"

"You guys want to help me with a side gig? It's a weird one. Came by actual mail. That should tell you something."

He dumps the folded sheets of paper from the torn end of the envelope and begins to read aloud, trailing off as Simon moves to stand behind him.

"Dear...wait, how does he know your real name?"

"Right?"

You have to stop us. We're going to kill again. I know what you're doing. The list. Put me on the list. Don't tell me. You can't tell me what to do. It's bad. It's bad. It's wrong. He makes me do it with him. Stop. Too many years. Too many. Dead. Too many. It's not my fault. He says we have to because they're bad. He's lying to us. All of us. I told him to stop. We all told him to stop. He never sleeps. Don't forget. Milk, eggs, butter, coffee, sourdough. Don't forget. He's strong. Too strong. We'll have to fight. You and me and him. We all have to fight. But you can't make me. Professional help. Professional. Processional. Perversional. Conversional. Stop, go, wait. What does he look like what what what?? The picture. Send the picture. Picture this. Say cheese. Cheeserito. Go, hurry. He's here.

On the following page is a pencil drawing of a middle-aged man. It's good, not cartoony like you might find on the boardwalk or at the fair. On par with a forensic artist. In the same deliberately neat handwriting found throughout the letter, an address is written across the forehead of the man in the sketch. Carlin and Simon stare at me, presumably waiting for an explanation.

"Okay, weird, right? But check this out. I googled the name, obviously." Pulling out my phone, I open it to a website about a forty-year-old cold-case. The name on the letter matches the name of one of the victims. "Strange coincidence, yeah?" Swiping up on the screen, an image appears. Another sketch of what looks like the same man, this one drawn by a police artist. Not identical, but not far off.

"Okay, but that's not the craziest part. All of *these* crimes happened thirty, forty years ago. I started doing searches for other similar cases on the west coast. Similar M.O. for over thirty other murders through the eighties and nineties. Gay men disappearing after visiting a nightclub. All found stabbed to death a day or two later. Every few months for, what, almost thirty years? Then, nothing. If these are all the same person, or people, what happened? Did he change his routine? Move away?" They stare at my phone as I swipe through screenshots of a couple dozen cold-case reports.

The door handle clicks and I hurriedly shove the letter and my phone into my pocket. Zaya notices as she enters the room, but doesn't say anything.

"Hey. We were just going to say hi to the guys next door," I stammer. Carlin knocks, then pulls open the door, revealing an identical room. Our enclaves quickly homogenize as musicians and their girlfriends amble between rooms. Monica calls for the first band and they file out through our dressing room, stage left, carrying guitars and drum sticks and offering high-fives or fist-bumps to those of us staying behind. Their girlfriends exit at the far door and disappear down the ramp and corridor to the theater.

The ritual repeats as the first band returns and is replaced on the stage by the next. We can stand in the wings of the stage to watch, but there aren't seats for us in the audience. Three rows back, Zaya sits with the other girlfriends and wives who were backstage. She sees me standing behind the curtains and waves subtly from her lap. I return the gesture before retreating backstage for another beer.

Playing in front of a seated audience is always weird. You can never tell if they're bored or not. The cheers and applause are louder, more enthusiastic, than at a club, but in between, flat. An occasional whistle during a guitar solo. Personally, I like to just sit quietly and watch live music, but it all seems so unnatural from the stage. They sit and stare at us for four minutes, followed by twenty seconds of clapping, another four minutes of staring.

Clap, stare, clap, stare. An unplugged set would make more sense. Make the show a little more intimate and personal.

Another beer and bump after the set, then we help pack up and haul out the gear that was shared with us tonight. I flip my collar up and button my jacket. It's easily thirty degrees colder outside than in our dressing room. My nose is running and freezing over at the same time. The cold air feels refreshing as it rushes through my recently-stimulated nostril.

We're invited to stay the night in the rehearsal space of the other band. It's just a few couches, surrounded by amps and drums – once we've helped them bring their equipment in – but it's heated. Chris and Jesse take them up on the offer. The rest of us will stay in the RV, hopefully not burning through all of our propane in the process. We could drive through the night, as we've been doing, but parking the rig discreetly in San Francisco would be impossible. They probably don't have Walmart parking lots in the city.

Before calling it a night, we congregate in the rehearsal space, trading licks with our hosts and doing lines off a light-box one of the guys keeps around for photography work. Our attempts at a jam session drift aimlessly from style to style. With such a diverse group of musicians in the room, nobody can stay focused on one song for too long.

The band tells us we can leave the RV in the parking lot of the rehearsal space tonight, showing us where to plug in an extension cord and hose, if we need them. They want to meet up for breakfast in the morning, but I'm not sure, I tell them. We need to hit the road pretty early. The guitar player points to the next street over and says to hit up the cafe before we leave. They live just up that street. Then he turns to catch up with his friends, already walking in that direction.

I pull the gig bags from the loft, letting Zaya up ahead of me. We say our goodnights and close the curtain. I hear bunk curtains sliding closed across the cabin.

"Seems like an exciting life," Zaya whispers as she snuggles up next to me.

"Eh. I guess. If you're doing it every day. We don't do this often, so it's more like vacation. To be honest, it gets exhausting fast."

"You're telling me. What do you do the rest of the time?"

"Oh, I don't know, read, write, play with the dogs, stay sober. Pretty much the exact opposite of what I do on tour."

"That sounds nice." She's silent for several breaths. "Do you want to talk about your book? I finished it."

"Uh, no, not really. Not ever. I don't know if I should have written that stuff or not. Or, at least, not published it."

"I think it's good. Genius." Genius. Special. Magical. Indigo. People have said these things to me all my life. I don't get it. Makes me uncomfortable. If I'm so special, then why all the bullshit in my life. I feel more cursed than anything. Nobody ever calls me that.

"You should do those things you wrote about. The arcade and stuff."

"Yeah, should. I should do a lot of things." I haven't told her yet about my illness. About the brain hole. Depression. It's nice to have someone look at me as a regular person for a while, before their perception is permanently colored. She made it through my book, including three entire journals written while I was locked up in the crazy house. That has to mean something.

"Oh, I'm so sorry," she says, squeezing me tighter as I tell her about the problems I've been having lately. How it's frustrating and maddening to lose my mind a little bit at a time. Learning not to take for granted simple things, like being able to drive a car.

"That explains the suicide note."

"That's not exactly what that was. More like a non-suicide note. Writing instead of killing myself. An alternative, not a predecessor."

"You're right, you know. It's wrong to force someone to live their life in pain. If I were suffering like that, I'd want to die, too." After a long pause, her head rising up and down on my chest as I breathe, she continues, "It's pretty fucked up. It kinda makes me angry. All those people and what they did to you. If I were you, I would never trust anyone again."

I chuckle under my breath. Without speaking again, we fall asleep.

"I've never been here before."

Zaya is staring out the passenger window, sitting in front with me as I pay the toll and start across the bridge. Fog still hangs low over the city, taking its time to burn off in the late-morning sun. It isn't until we're nearly across the bay that the skyline of the city appears in front of us.

"I'll have to show you around tomorrow," I tell her. Right now we've gotta make up some time.

Instead of going to the hotel, I drop Simon and Carlin at the Enterprise nearest the freeway and continue on to the venue. It's in a shit neighborhood and I don't like leaving all our stuff here, but there's no way I'm driving this thing to the hotel. I've stayed there before and it'll never fit in their little car-port. There are parking garages nearby, but I don't feel like circling the block a dozen times to find one we can fit in.

I'm starting to roll down the security screen and lock up when Simon pulls up next to us in a white CRV.

"Sorry, it's the biggest they had," he says out the window as it rolls down. Instead of trying to cram all of us and our gear in, we opt for two trips. I send Zaya ahead with Simon and Carlin, passing my credit card to the front seat as I kiss her through the open door.

As they drive away, Chris, Jesse, and I fold the metal stairs out and climb back inside to crank the heater. Jesse starts cutting out lines on the table while I warm up the Keurig for Irish coffee. May as well, we're going to be here a while.

"Did you guys know that this whole area we're in right now is made of trash, just piled into the water until they could build on it?"

"Dude, what's with you taking us to places that could

suddenly explode or fall into the ocean?"

"Technically, on this side of the city, it's a bay," I smirk, setting mugs on the table in front of them and spooning fresh whipped cream on top.

The latch clicks and Simon reaches through the door, retrieving the last suitcase. Finishing what's left on the table, we follow him to the idling Honda. Chris helps me pull down and latch the security gate for a second time.

"Not such a fancy place, mate," Simon says as he pulls away from the RV.

"The club or the hotel?"

"Both, actually."

"Not at first, but you'll see. They aren't without their charm."

The first charming thing about the old motor lodge at the bottom of the hill is the price. Less than a hundred bucks a night. In San Francisco. It's also within walking distance of the Presidio and the Marina District.

I hear beeps and buzzes through the doors after I send a group text from our third-floor hallway, telling everyone to come out of their rooms. Zaya opens the door closest to me and wraps her arms around me, kissing me until we hear another door open. She doesn't put her tongue in my mouth when she kisses me like this. Not like when we're having sex.

Our party assembled, I open the heavy emergency exit at the end of the hall and wave everyone up the stairs. The alarm doesn't sound. It never does. When you think about it, an emergency exit going *up* doesn't make a lot of sense. I mean, if the place is on fire and you can't get down, sure, but if that's the case the fire department is already going to be looking for people on the roof and there's no need for an alarm. I'm sure it's just a deterrent.

From the roof above our rooms, we can see what seems like the entire city. The Golden Gate to one side, towering skyscrapers to the other. This is the real reason I stay at this hotel. Holding out the cardboard six-pack container, everyone grabs a bottle and we gaze across the bay, the sun already starting to sag toward the Pacific. I have to help Zaya open her beer with a lighter, she doesn't know how to do it.

A quick shower and costume change later, the six of us cram into the four-and-a-half seats of the CRV for the trek across town to the gig.

"Goddammit, Jesse. You're staying here!" Chris shouts as Jesse leans across, searching beneath himself for the elusive middle seatbelt. I do my best to share the right third of the back seat with Zaya, neither one of us wearing a seatbelt. Jesse, still searching, falls on top of us as Simon thuds over the curb from the covered parking area and onto the slick road. I tell him to take Van Ness, just ahead or we'll end up on the curvy section of Lombard. The rabble sitting next to me thinks this would be a good idea, but I insist we don't have time for that today.

"Tomorrow. We can do whatever you guys want tomorrow. I think we're going to stay another day. You can take the rig and we'll take the train back unless you all want to stay?"

After some discussion, we arrive in front of the club, now lit in neon, illuminating the dark industrial-residential neighborhood in an array of color. A decision still hasn't been made. I offer the keys as the six of us walk across the street and Carlin takes them from me, diverging toward the RV, leaving me walking alone to the entrance of the venue.

I show the bouncer my ID without being asked and point toward the RV, where he can't see, but can probably hear, the band unloading equipment.

"Are they all twenty-one?"

"Yeah, brother. Most of us twice-over."

"How many?"

"Six."

He counts out six wristbands. Purple with the letter 'H'.

Different from the tall stack of blue, Bud-Light wristbands on the cocktail table next to him. Inside, he tells me, there's pizza and apps by the kitchen entrance and we can help ourselves.

Passing out the wristbands and repeating the offer of food, I pick up a couple of gig bags and head back to the club, again alone, nodding to the bouncer as I enter. Normally, it would be the road manager's job to go inside, meet the staff, figure out the game plan. If we had roadies, I'd let Jesse do it, but in this case, he can move the gear. I've played here before, anyway.

The headlining act is in from out of town and on rented equipment. They've offered to let us use whatever we want. Whenever one band says this to another band, they mean amps and drums, usually. Guitars, cymbals, sticks and, often, kick pedals aren't included in the offer. It's a two-way courtesy.

The guys come in, dragging wheelie-cases, bundled with gig bags. "You can probably take some of that back," I say, pointing them toward the stage. "Where's Zaya?"

"Waiting with the rest of the stuff."

"Really, guys? You leave her alone in a neighborhood like this?"

"We figured it was that or make her carry all this shit." I can't argue with the logic. It's like risking getting stuck in a storm because we'd rather have Chris shit in the gas station.

Outside, I grab the last couple of things we'll need for soundcheck and lock the doors, escorting Zaya back to the venue. I can hear the band already pounding through one of our songs, checking their levels. Simon shuffles through sound patches on the two-tiered keyboard setup.

Pointing Zaya toward the kitchen, I climb to the stage and flip open the latches on my tweed guitar case. I think I'll bring the Tele out from its usual role as a backup tonight. The orange glow of the tubes gradually lights up the black curtain behind my amp. Alternating between soft rhythm parts and distorted leads, I'm dialed in with the sound guy in about sixty seconds. We play through three-quarters of one of our songs to let him fine-tune the mix, stopping when he clicks onto our monitors and tells us we're good.

The stage riser is eight feet above the dance floor, that's the first nice thing about this venue. The free food and drinks are always a plus, too. I lead our entourage to the back patio, a secluded garden, replete with planters, benches, and ivy-covered walls. A hidden sanctuary in the middle of a metropolitan mecca.

We pass around a blunt, taking hits between puffs on our cigarettes. The patio is empty now, with doors not opening for another twenty minutes. Honestly, I don't know if anyone would care about us smoking weed out here when the venue *is* open. San Francisco is supposed to be pretty chill about that, but at the same time, never underestimate the cops in California. A security guard sits by himself on a stool near the bottom of a wooden staircase.

"C'mon. Put that out. This is what I actually wanted to show you out here," I say, walking toward the bouncer. Folding up my sleeve, I show him the purple wristband and he unlatches the chain, checking each wristband as we pass him to ascend the narrow steps.

Inside the small apartment, we introduce ourselves to the other group, who surround a foosball table, slamming the rods hard enough to lift the legs from the ground. An ice chest overflows with bottled beers bearing the same logo as our wristbands. Rice lager. Turning the bottle over, I see the address on the label is just down the street.

Chris and Simon both know all about this band. They've been looking forward to this gig all tour. All month. I saw them once. Shit, fifteen years ago? They were opening for Dream Theater at some crazy upstairs club not far from here. I got punched in the throat by a lone 'mosher' and ended up spending most of Dream Theater's set outside. My friend and I met these guys in the plaza as they were getting ready to leave. They wouldn't remember me. I don't recognize them, either. It was a long time ago. I'd guess they've changed some members since then.

Trying not to be too fanboy, Chris and Simon chat up the players of their respective instruments. These guys are crazy talented. It's prog-rock, so they have to be, but they put on a great live show, too.

Jesse offers some freshly cut cocaine around the room. The other band declines, saying they can't get too fucked up before a gig. Makes sense. Their music is far more complicated than the four-chord stuff we play. They continue to pound cocktails. It's funny how everyone sets their own arbitrary limits. Cocaine is too much, but a liter of hard liquor is okay. Some guys will drink day and night, but refuse pot because it gets them too fucked up. Blows my mind. Then again, you wouldn't catch me eating mushrooms anywhere near a gig. Never again.

There's a knock on the glass of the door before it swings open. The security guard points to the bottom of the stairs, where the chain is still fastened. A man with shaggy, salt-and-pepper hair and a cabbie hat stands below, waving when he sees my head pop out from behind the door frame.

"Oh, shit! What the fuck?" I yell down the stairs, giving the okay to the security guard to give him a purple wristband.

"Guys, this is Kyle. You never met, but he's on the album." I offer him a bump from what's left on the tray. Carlin escorts him to the counter, opening a drawer in the kitchenette to let Kyle select a straw in a paper wrapper.

"You don't see these around here much anymore," he says, cutting the straw in half with a pair of scissors and bending over to take a hit with each nostril.

"You bring your axe?" I ask, handing him a whiskey-rocks. "Sorry, no scotch up here."

"Yeah, dude, it's in the car." Abandoning the drink on the counter, he opens a beer.

"Right on. Jump up there with us if you're feeling it."

Another knock and the door opens an inch or two. "Ten

minutes, The Walls Instead," the security guard calls through the crack in the door. Stuffing beers in our coat pockets, we offer our thanks to the other band for the backline and hang. Outside, we have time for one more smoke before downbeat. The patio is crowded now.

Turns out, Kyle is feeling it from the start. He joins us for the second song and stays on for the rest of the set. Another couple of songs in and the sound tech runs on stage, crouched over like people might notice him less, and plugs in another mic for the trumpet. I'll have to remember to thank and apologize to him later. Simon turns the boom stand back around so he can back up Carlin on the chorus. Since he doesn't know the material, I try to pass as many leads and solos off to Kyle as possible. He did play on a couple tunes on the album, but I wouldn't expect him to remember the parts. I don't remember what I played on his album. It adds a nice variety to the set, having a second soloist. And after playing the same licks for the last week, I need a break from guitar solos as much as anyone else.

We hang around, mostly in the club, for the entirety of the next act, venturing back upstairs every couple of songs for a fresh beer or a pick-me-up. We're not getting wasted; each song is like twelve-minutes long. Chris and Simon stand on the side of the stage-riser for most of the ninety-minute set. Sadly, the kitchen is closed and the hospitality trays from earlier have long-since gone.

After their second encore, we hang out for a couple more drinks 'backstage', or whatever the apartment would be called. Kyle smuggles up a bottle of Laphroaig-10 in his trumpet case and is immediately dismayed at my band's propensity for taking shots of it. With the unsoiled half of his straw from earlier, he drips water from a plastic bottle into the lowball glass he brought from home.

With no more action going on downstairs, I presume the staff wants to get us out so they can go home. I'd rather they didn't have to ask us. Announcing to the room that we need to go, everyone stands and says their goodbyes. They seem a bit tipsy, so I remind my players to check and double-check the stage for any gear before we go. The venue stands empty again, save for two staff members. Same as when we got here, but the lights are off now.

"Thanks for having us, guys," I say as the bouncer opens the door. The rain has started again. We run for the RV, unable to pull our jackets over our heads with gig bags on our shoulders. I struggle to get the slick metal screen unlocked and rolled up.

We don't even bother to turn on the lights. Just toss our instruments into the loft and lock it back up for the night. Simon is pulling the micro-SUV around to the empty space in front of us. Long night, long tour. Zaya and I have our own private room tonight.

"What can we eat around here?" Jesse asks from the middle hump of the back seat.

"Mel's is open late, I think. Right down the street from the hotel." I don't remember eating much today, but I'm not hungry. We retire to our room for the evening. She's drunk from the scotch, beer, and whatever else she had when we were on stage.

I open the door and help her in. She needs help undressing and going pee. Not going pee, obviously, but getting to the toilet. I support her as she stumbles wildly from the bathroom to our bed. I throw back the covers and lift her feet onto the mattress, climbing in beside her with my clothes still on.

"Happy Valentine's Day," she mumbles, barely audible. Within seconds, her breathing changes. She's asleep. Shit, I totally forgot today was Valentine's Day.

A few minutes later, I'm sneaking out.

She's passed out until morning, I'd bet. If she wakes up, she'll call before looking for me. I'll just tell her we went midnight sight-seeing around the city.

The diner is too brightly-lit for this time of night. Every surface glows white. The floors, the ceilings, the employee uniforms, all white. Only some of these things are actually white. My eyes must still be adjusting.

I pull a stray chair from an empty table up to the two-tone booth where the band is sitting, spinning it around, to lean over the backrest. "Sup, dudes?" I pick stray fries from the plates scattered around the table, using them to sop up gravy from around what's left of Carlin's hot, open-faced turkey sandwich. "You don't want that?" I ask Chris, pointing at the pickle spear on his plate. He shakes his head and holds the plate up at me. I stab at the pickle with a fresh fork and eat it in two bites.

"I thought you were going to bed?"

"Meh. Zaya's drunk and I'm still awake. I could take another bump." Chris and Jesse are starting to look tired. Jesse taps at my knee with a glass vial under the table. "I'm good, bro. I have my own."

Dropping a hundred on the table for their tab, I stand and put my jacket back on, following the band onto the sidewalk. We power-walk in the rain back to the hotel and take the stairs up to the third floor. I wait in the hallway, not wanting to risk waking Zaya, as they disappear into their rooms. A few moments later, Simon and Carlin emerge and we're on our way back down the stairs, en route to the parking lot.

"Shit, I think this is the freeway," Simon says, cutting across the empty road to make a sudden left at the green light.

"Wait, are you sure this doesn't go into the park?"

"I don't know. The map says this is a highway," he says, pointing at the GPS-slash-stereo in the center of the dash. It's a digital map, but we have to navigate the old-fashioned way, without leaving behind a search history.

"This guy is a ghost. Or guys," I explain as we come out of the other side of the park to what is clearly still not a freeway. "I matched a name to the address. Sixty-eight-year-old male. No social media, no public records."

"What do you want to do?" Carlin asks, leaning in from the back seat.

"Fuck, I have no idea. Let's just scope the place out and see what we're dealing with."

"You armed?" Simon asks, looking away from the road at each of us. We both produce pocketknives and show them to him.

"Fucking blades, man. Too messy."

"What about that ricin stuff?" He glares at me. I know as I'm speaking that I shouldn't have let it slip in front of Carlin.

"It wasn't ricin, but either way, I only had the one. Not something you want to be carrying around with you, y'know?" I want to ask him about the taser device, but I've already said too much. As far as Carlin knows, or knew, I was just asking Simon along for an extra hand, a driver maybe.

The road we're on does eventually become a freeway, but not for long before we're merging over to the off-ramp. Simon races down the hill, into the neighborhood. The streets are narrow and deserted. As the road levels out, we're struggling to read the dimly-lit addresses posted next to the front doors of the green, pink, and beige stucco houses.

"Right here, five-thirty-seven," Carlin says, tapping on the window to his left. Simon continues on to the next intersection, making a u-turn and pulling in a few houses down, wheels on the curb, like the few other cars lining the one-lane street.

"Cat's out of the bag now," Simon says, pulling a black

nylon case from the cargo area and passing us each an in-ear monitor. Not a monitor, I guess, since it's two-way, but that's what I'm used to calling them. We're twisting them into our ears when he hands us each a small-caliber pistol, silencer equipped.

"Only if you absolutely have to. It's still plenty loud."

Carlin is looking at us from the back seat, clearly bewildered. "Don't ask," I say. "Not tonight."

Walking casually and quietly through the neighborhood, I climb over the concrete wall and into the back yard. Carlin unlatches the unlocked gate and follows me behind the house.

"Okay, I've got a good view through the front windows," Simon says through my earpiece. "It's dark on this side of the house, looks like there's a light on in the back. A kitchen, maybe."

A dog barks viciously as we come around the corner, onto the back patio. We startle and prepare to run, but notice the barking is coming from the other side of the fence. Hunching over, we Chuck-Berry walk away from the dog and under the darkened windows to the edge of the glass doors, where we can see a light on.

"Anything?" Simon asks.

"Neighbor's dog. Nothing inside."

We wait several minutes, listening to the silence coming from the house before deciding to cross in front of the transparent doors, to the kitchen window. Looking at each other, we nod and make a run for it, crashing into each other and into the patio chairs before falling to the ground. We both saw it. The tall, skinny man standing at the back door, staring out through the glass.

Shaking our heads to clear the temporary disorientation, we both look over to the window for confirmation. I freeze and Carlin turns white. He's still there. Just staring at us. Not moving. Nobody moves. Nobody blinks.

"What the fuck was that?" Simon asks. We don't respond. Carlin is discreetly reaching for his gun. Slowly. Slower. Almost not moving at all.

"It's dark," I whisper, putting my hand on top of his. "Maybe he can't see us out here."

The next ten seconds feel like an hour as we sit motionless, staring back at the shadowy figure. Inside the house, the doorbell rings and the man turns and totters towards the front of the house. The moment his back is turned, we sprint for the side-yard on the opposite side of the house, sitting on the cold, wet concrete under the one illuminated window.

"Thanks, mate," I say to the air in front of me.

"No worries. Just needed a little knick-knocking," my earpiece says back. "He's back on your side now."

Turning around, I lean back in an attempt to see through the kitchen window. Just cabinets and lights. Standing, I press myself against the wall and peek through the glass. Carlin stands on the other side. Between the two of us, we should be able to see the entire kitchen.

"See anything?" He asks. I squint and shake my head, not in the negative, but unsure what I'm looking at. It's the same man, naked except a white afghan blanket draped over his shoulders, walking to the refrigerator, opening the door, staring in with surprise or disgust, closing the door, turning to face the wall, then turning back and opening the door to the fridge again. Over and over, never changing his movements, never varying his reaction to whatever is inside.

"He just keeps looking in the fridge."

"What?" Carlin whispers.

"What?" my earpiece echoes in a different voice.

"I know you're there," the man says, expressionless. Carlin and I freeze, pressed against the stucco, holding our breath.

"It's not your time. No. No. Don't talk to me like that." He's not talking to us. Breaking away from the refrigerator, he paces back and forth in the kitchen, shuffling his feet through the crumpled newspaper and soup cans that litter the floor.

"They know about you. I told on you. They know. They

know. They know. They know," he keeps repeating this to himself as he paces four steps in one direction, then the other, making big, round circles as he turns.

"Is it the right guy?" Simon asks. "Are you sure?" I nod, forgetting that he can't hear me.

"Yeah, same as the drawing." He freezes and stares out the window when I say this. Unblinking, his pacing stopped, he looks blankly out the window into the darkness.

"Drawing. What drawing? Those are mine. How dare you steal from me!" He resumes his pacing. Four steps, turn in a circle, four steps the opposite direction.

"What in the literal fuck, dude?" Carlin whispers across the window.

"Okay, I'm coming back there."

Simon walks casually across the back yard, crouching only slightly as he approaches our post at the corner of the house.

"Just get away from me. You're dirty. Dirty. Bad man. Dirty bad man." The pacing in the kitchen continues.

"I have an idea," Simon whispers. "I don't know, could be crazy. Any other ideas besides run-n-gun?"

"Dude, I'm at a fuckin' loss. Whatever you think, let's do it." Carlin stares through the window at the man pacing and talking to himself while Simon and I discuss his plan in whispers, the rain soaking through our shirts, under our coats.

"I don't know, man. You're serious?"

"He clearly doesn't know what the fuck is going on. We should take advantage of that."

"Okay, let's go."

We creep around the side of the house and let ourselves out through the gate and into the driveway. Strolling to the front door, Simon rings the bell. He stands there, soaking wet, looking bored, waiting for the door to open.

"Good evening, sir. I'm sorry to bother you. We're here to repair your cable."

"Oh, did I call? I must have. Thank you for coming so fast. Three of you? There must be a real problem."

"Nothing serious," Simon says, tilting his head to indicate we should go inside. "We should have it fixed in no time."

"Isn't that so kind of you. I'm here all alone, you know. It gets so lonely, don't you know? Nobody coming to call on me anymore."

"I'll tell you what," Simon says to the old man, patting him on the hand. "We'll give you the extra movie channels at no cost, okay?"

Not bothering to cover himself with the afghan, the man appears to get aroused at Simon's touch. Upon noticing, his excitement changes to embarrassment. Anger? I can't tell. He rushes off to the kitchen.

"Dude, it's like two in the morning. How is this not suspicious?" Carlin whispers from behind the old projection TV. The rabbit ears on top of the VCR make it clear that this house doesn't even have cable service.

"TV repair? TV Repair?? That can't be right. Who called?" We all freeze, listening to the voice coming from the kitchen. "I can tell you right now, I didn't call for any repairmen. What time is it?"

"Shit, should we go?" Carlin asks, still pretending to fix the wires on the back of the television.

"They're not even wearing uniforms. What kind of idiot do you take me for? That's it, I've had enough! I'm just going to cancel the whole plan." Simon picks up the cordless landline phone from the end table next to him and presses the button. We can all hear the dial tone.

"Still talking to himself," Simon whispers. "Hang here for a minute. Just distract him if he comes back." We say nothing, unsure what the hell to do with this guy when he does come back and certain that we should have never come here in the first place. We're way out of our league. He might seem like a crazy old man, but if he's who we think he is, he wouldn't hesitate to kill us.

The door on the opposite side of the living room rests against the door frame, closed but not latched. A few seconds later, we hear the sound of an engine turning over and idling on the other side of that door. A truck or maybe an old muscle car.

"What was that? Did you hear that?" The man comes into the living room, blanket and flaccid dong swaying in unison as he rounds the corner and looks around the room, searching. There's no mistaking the sound of the engine coming from just a few feet away, yet he looks behind chairs and on bookcases, kicking trash out of his way as he moves.

"Did one of you break something? It's okay. I won't be mad if you did." We both shake our heads, trying not to make eye contact with any part of him, but keeping him in our periphery in case his demeanor changes.

"Okay, all finished," Simon announces, closing the door to the garage behind him, as if that's where he was supposed to come from.

The man stops Simon at the doorway, letting Carlin and I pass by, into the rain, to wait in the driveway. "Honey, I hate to be the one to tell you this, but I think one of your workers broke something in there. I heard a noise, but I can't find it."

"Oh, I'm so sorry," Simon says with genuine compassion. "I hope this will cover it." He passes a folded hundred-dollar bill into the man's wrinkled, trembling fingers and turns toward the driveway.

"You are just the nicest young man. I'm going to call your boss and tell him you deserve a big raise. Such a good boy. Don't you worry about those floors, neither. I'll just go clean those muddy footprints up right now. Such a good boy. You come back and see me any time, okay?"

Simon waves over his shoulder as we reconvene outside of the exterior garage door, engine still idling inside. He leads us back to the rental, starting the motor and pulling out from the narrow row of parked cars.

"So?"

"That's it, mate. Well, almost. One more stop and we can get some sleep. You know, I think I will stay another night with you. What do you think, B?"

"Dude, I'm so fucking confused about what happened right now. Can we talk about it in the morning?"

"No worries. We'll wake you up when we get back to the motel."

As the freeway turns back into city streets, and we enter San Francisco proper, Simon winds through a commercial neighborhood, past darkened boutiques and convenience stores at a snail's pace.

"What are you looking for?"

"Payphone."

"Probably will have better luck up by the park. The Haight." He follows the road back around to the thoroughfare and starts north again. Sure enough, right at the west end of the park, we spot a phone kiosk, still fully intact, next to a bus bench.

Carlin doesn't stir when Simon pulls to the curb, puts on a pair of latex gloves, and runs to the payphone, slamming the door behind him. He inserts several coins and dials a number. Waiting, looking into the car at me, he hangs up the receiver, withdraws his change from the return, filtering it back into the slot at the top, and dials again. This time I see him say something, then set the handset on top of the phone without hanging it up.

"Okay, *now* we're done." The dome light fades, he puts the transmission back into drive and the tires slip slightly as he merges back onto the empty street.

I'm tired, too. Carlin wakes up as we stop at the light in front of our hotel. It's strange how our bodies do that. Know how to wake up at the right time. We groggily climb the stairs, our shoes making sloshing and sucking noises as we tread over carpeted steps.

In my room, I peel off my wet clothes and stuff them in a plastic bag, then into the bottom pocket of my suitcase. Zaya doesn't look like she's moved at all since I left. Shallow breathing. Gentle snoring. I let the rhythm of her breath coax me to sleep.

Steam fogs the transparent glass.

We all watch is awe as the bartender pours coffee and booze into a five-foot-long line of clear mugs before topping them with cream and passing them to us.

"Hey, this tastes familiar," Chris jokes, wiping the milky foam from his mustache. The white paper napkin curls and turns brown as he sets the clear mug back on the bar.

"Yeah, where do you think I stole it from!" Ornate tile frames carved oak on nearly every surface. This bar has the best Irish coffee. Of course I 'borrowed' their recipe. Typically, I don't use Tully. Too hard to find. Any cheap Irish whiskey will do the trick.

Carlin wants to stop by the Irish pub for a beer before we continue our walking-tour of the city. It's only ten a.m. and we're on our third drink of the day. Zaya and I were up with the sunrise, sitting in silence on the hotel roof, sipping coffee, breathing in the city. Even with our late night, everyone was up and ready to check out before nine. I reminded them I was going to stay and they all decided to renew their rooms for another night.

Dinner rolls and sauerkraut wasn't what I expected to have for breakfast. Piling a heaping ladle of cabbage atop the bread, I cough as the steam hits my nose. I've always had a bit of a sensitivity to vinegar. Zaya tells me it's cute how I cough a little with each bite. I wouldn't be eating the stuff, but I'm already feeling warm and a little bleary-eyed from the whiskey. I'll have to fill my belly if I expect to keep this up for another twelve or fifteen hours.

We sit at the bar, sipping our lager. Carlin is browsing the local news on his phone, looking for something about last night, I bet. Glancing over his shoulder, I don't see anything.

"Technically, it was Daly City," I murmur, almost inaudibly. He searches for Daly City news. Nothing. He sticks his phone back in his jacket and stands up, finishing his beer. I toss the soppy mess on my paper plate into the bin and leave a twenty on the bar before following the group back out to the street. Nice weather today. No fog, no rain. It's cold, but not Oregon-in-a-snow-storm cold.

Circling the block, we stop for ice cream. I don't have any. That's the last thing I need. A bunch of milk and sugar on top of whiskey and fermented cabbage. Zaya insists on sharing her hot-fudge-sundae-in-a-cone with me. I have a bite to be polite, but avoid any future offers. Too much sugar and I'll be puking before lunch.

We stroll in two groups around the neighborhood, finishing dessert, peering into shop windows. Zaya stops and pulls a pink-and-black paisley scarf from one of the racks that leans out onto the sidewalk. She says she has to buy it for me.

Wrapping it around my neck, she uses it to pull me in for a kiss, then we jog to catch up to the guys, who are disappearing into the spy shop. Several items are admired and played with, but no purchases are made. It's novelty stuff, mostly. Nanny cams, oversized glasses in a style nobody would wear unless they were trying to hide a camera. Nothing a real spy would use. Or maybe they would.

On the pier, we have oyster shots, swallowing the slimy mollusks whole with our peppered vodka or spiced tequila. Even Zaya has one, for the new experience. She gags and makes a sickly face, chewing the oyster as she tries to force herself to swallow.

"That was the most disgusting thing I've ever had," she exhales. Everyone else finds this hilarious and orders another round. The bar, like the rest of the pier, is mostly deserted. Hardly any performers line the Embarcadero. A silver statue dude, a guy with a guitar, that's about it.

More walking. Up Telegraph Hill, turning haphazardly this way and that on the narrow streets. I'd hate to have to drive through this neighborhood. The architecture changes, gradually at first, then all of a sudden. Chinatown.

Discount stores, big and small, sell everything imaginable at a fraction of the price we're used to seeing, even in stores like Walmart. Clothes, cookware, toys, trinkets. Chris wants to buy a sword, but I remind him that there's no tang, so he can't cut anything with it. Plus, he'll have to lug it around the city all day.

Down the street, we stop for another beer at the Buddha Bar, one of my favorite dives. No matter what city you're in, dive bars all have that same stale, acidic smell. Piss, vomit, spilled drinks. They all come together to create an aroma as unmistakable as an Abercrombie store.

"Dude, that basement looks like it was built to be a torture chamber," Carlin says, coming up the stairs from the restroom.

"I know, right?"

Chris, Jesse, and Simon get up from their seats and venture into the stairwell to see for themselves. Their voices and laughter echo off the concrete walls to the bar. Coming back up, and without sitting down, they finish their green-bottled beers and we continue our trek.

Another mile down Broadway, Jesse decides he's tired of walking and pages a ride big enough for our group. A dented Dodge Caravan. The door slides open as it pulls to the curb and we pile onto the stained bench seats. Carlin opens the front door and lets himself in.

"What's up, man? We don't know where we want to go. Any recommendations?" Carlin says, turning to the driver, starting to slur.

"Yeah, bro. Where you from, bro?"

"Here," Carlin responds. "California."

"You been to the pier? Golden Gate Park, bro?"

"Yeah," I say from the back seat. "No more touristy shit.

Take us somewhere weird."

"Okay, bro." The driver adjusts his mirror to look back at me. "I know just the place."

Yevhen, that's our driver's name, but he says we can call him 'Gene' if we want, is from Ukraine. He's lived here for three years. Not here, in San Francisco, he tells us, the east bay.

"Ukraine?" Zaya asks. "Where about? I have family from Poland." I didn't know this about her. I avoid asking people about their genealogy almost universally. If they aren't white, I worry they'll get upset, like it's a racist question. Some people would rather not talk about their families at all, regardless of race.

"No. No, not close. Sevastopol. Far from Poland."

"Is that like the town north of here?" Carlin asks.

"Yeah, bro. Sebastopol is named after my hometown."

"You wouldn't rather live there?"

"Sonoma county is too expensive, bro. It's not like home, anyway, you know, bro?" Looking over his shoulder, Yevhen swerves toward the curb and slams on the brakes, fitting neatly between the parallel-parked cars in front of and behind us.

"This is it, bro," he says, pointing at the narrow storefront, painted in faux-ivy. "I'll wait here, yeah? You guys want to party?"

"Fuck yeah!" Chris calls back as he climbs out of the van.

When I asked for weird, maybe I should have been more specific. Taxidermied animal heads of every shape and size line the walls. Bleached bones and dehydrated sea-creatures fill bins on one side of us. At the far end, the room opens up to a variety of plants. All green. All living. I'm not an advocate for the display of murdered animals. Growing up, my uncle's dad, my aunt's father-in-law, no relation, had animal heads and body parts throughout his house. It used to terrify me as a child, especially the elephant-foot foot-stool they would tell me to sit on. It has a different energy here. The animals aren't being displayed as trophies. They aren't bragging about their ability to kill things.

After adequately fondling the various curiosities, we file out, being careful not to break anything on our way. Yevhen is waiting in front of the expired meter, engine idling.

"Pretty sick. Right, bros?"

"It was definitely weird, good job there. How about somewhere with less dead animals next?"

"Sure thing, bro. Your girlfriend will like the next one."

Emerging from under the freeway, we pass several big-box retailers with actual parking lots. Something found on every street corner back home feels foreign and wrong here. Otherwise, the view on our drive is quintessential San Francisco. Three-and-four story buildings crowd the street, their bay windows dangling precariously above the sidewalk.

We stand under one of these windows as our IDs are checked. The interior of the building is lit in purple and green LED, the lights hidden under clear plexiglass shelves and counters. The hostess hands us drink menus as we sit around the elongated cocktail table. Flipping the laminated menu over, I find more stupid, novelty drink names. Sake and a beer. I think I can order that without sounding like a fool. Do you think the first guy to order a vodka-orange juice from a plastic menu felt like a tool calling it a 'screwdriver'?

Dinner is served in courses and I don't have to say anything silly to order what I want. Tuna sashimi, soba with curried brussels sprouts and banana lumpia.

Before dessert is brought out, but after we've finished the second bottle of sake, the lights dim and canned music starts. Yevhen carries on telling us how much we're going to love this show and slapping us on the back, as he's been doing since we got here. He's increased in frequency and volume now that the sake has kicked in, turning his face deep red.

Judging by the glamour-shots pasted across the drink menu, I thought maybe we were in a strip club. I didn't look too hard. Turns out the lingerie-clad dancers on the bar and around our table are all men. Yevhen is in an uproar. Zaya buries her face in my shoulder, laughing hysterically. I'm not sure if this is meant to be funny. I'd hate to be rude to the performers. Jesse jumps up and grinds on one of the dancers for a brief moment before being escorted back to our table with a warning.

Ten hours of drinking and we're all still standing. Before moving on, we take turns going to the restroom, where Chris has left six generous rails on the back of a toilet. Zaya and I go together. This is all new to her, or so she says. I pass her a rolled bill and she snorts an entire line, coughing and gagging violently as she attempts to hand the twenty back to me. I tell her she's allowed to do it in more than one hit. She thanks me sarcastically.

Stuffing the tube in my left nostril, I take mine and prepare to clear out so the next person can use the stall. On our way out of the men's room, I point to the mirror and tease Zaya about the mascara tears running down her face.

I have enough energy for another stop. Wondering about live music, we cruise by the Fillmore, but it's dark, so we decide to check out the Castro. In front of me, in the middle seat, Carlin is searching the local news sites again. Still nothing, from what I can see.

We pop into a few bars for a drink, but never stay long. Most places open this late are too loud for my taste. They're all so crowded. I get it, we're in one of the largest metropolitan areas in the world, I should expect places to be crowded.

Below Market, we find a rustic bar with several unoccupied chairs and tables in the upstairs area. The lights and music are low. They're promoting their Irish coffee, too, but it's late for caffeine. Two cocktails later, it's last call and we're on our way back to the battered Caravan.

We give Yevhen a copy of our album and a generous tip when he drops us off at the bottom of Fillmore Street. Upstairs. Three flights. Shower, sex, smoke, sleep.

This is the end.

Our last day on tour. Technically, the tour ended on Sunday, but now we have to actually go home. With all the luggage, we have to take two trips back to the RV, still parked down the street from the venue, where we left it. Some asshole tagged the security door.

Zaya and I spend some time organizing the interior and cleaning before cuddling up together on the couch to wait for the band.

"You hungry?"

"Nah, not really," she says from my lap. "Make something if you want."

"I'm not hungry. I was going to make you breakfast if you were." She shakes her head and dozes off briefly, to be awakened by the door slamming against the side of the RV and the guys coming through like steamrollers. I try to shush them, but it's too late.

The atmosphere changes as we cross the bridge, heading east. We're all tired and ready to go home, but at the same time, nobody is quite ready to go back to regular life. The isolation and loneliness. It settles over us as we pass the banks of windmills, before we're even back to the 99. We watch the view out our windows flatten out to become farms and ranches.

"Everyone good?" I ask, picking up the empty cans from the table and replacing them with fresh ones.

"Hell yeah, man. Good times," Jesse says from the front. "Thanks for letting me come." It wasn't terrible having him play with us. More unnecessary than anything, given the format of our music. It's cool to have him along. I think Spiderweb wanted us to come by on our way back, I don't remember. It's out of our way now.

Checking the spreadsheet on my phone, I count out ten and twenty-dollar bills from the envelope under my seat and pass the stacks around the table. Jesse gets $500. It's not a full band cut. Not even a half-cut, but more than he was expecting, considering the meals, rooms and drinks we've been giving him all week. I've been ignoring my other spreadsheet all week. I kinda don't want to get back into it. My version of 'regular life'. It's a lot of work. A lot of crap to filter through. I'd rather just take it easy, hang around the house with Zaya, take naps in front of the fireplace. Plus, I can't really spend a lot of time on this side project with her hanging around if I want to keep it secret.

"Dude, I'm ready to go again. That was one of the best trips I've ever been on," Chris says, passing me his credit card to help myself to the pile he's dumped out in front of us.

"Want to try again?" I ask Zaya, scraping out the narrowest line I can. She shrugs and leans over my offering, holding a cocktail straw to her face. Looking up at me, her eyes are watering and she fans her face with her hand. At least she's not choking or vomiting. I help myself to a decidedly larger portion and pass the card back to Chris.

Simon scoops a key into the pile and holds it under his nose, sniffing loudly. Looking up, he says, "Yeah, I'm good any time, too. We did okay on the money this time, no?"

"Better than last time. Better each time, if we can keep expenses down." Most of the time, I pay for minor band expenses, like drinks, out of my own share. I don't tell them that, of course. I'd rather they made a little more and come away happier with the tour than worry about how much is being spent on alcohol.

Carlin is going to need a little more time to decompress and regroup before heading out on the road again. Same for me. I need at least a couple of months between tours anymore. I'm sure his wife doesn't appreciate him being gone so much, anyway. Any time musicians have families, tour schedules have to be approached delicately and infrequently. There's also a fine balance of travel time to gigs to days off. Too much travel between gigs and nobody has the time to enjoy the cities we're visiting. Not enough days off and players burn out. Too many days off and we lose money or get bored. For most bands, touring is losing money anyway. Until the audiences are in the thousands and all buying merchandise, the main goal is to break even and expose as many people to our music as possible.

I tell Jesse to exit the freeway before we get back to Fresno, so I can get my dogs. We load them into the cabin, muddy and jumping into each of our laps in turn. I introduce Zaya to Mizu, Lena, Yoshi and Charlie, the latter hiding under our feet, his tail thumping loudly against the wall.

"When we get home, you can meet Egg Ryan, Feather Locklear, Hennifer Aniston, Yolko Ono and the rest of the girls."

"What?" She looks at me, wrinkling her brow.

"Oh yeah," Chris says to her. "He likes to give all the animals weird names. Those aren't even the dog's full names. Just wait until he tells you the names of the lights."

"I don't even know what that means."

"Oh," I laugh. "I've got the whole smart-house thing set up. You know, like 'kitchen lights on' and stuff? Well, it's far more entertaining to name my electronics after dead child-stars. 'Hey Google, turn on Jonathan Brandis. Hey Google, play Steel Panther on Judith Barsi.'"

"Who and Who?"

At Jesse's, I try to keep the dogs inside while we unload, but inevitably, we end up having to chase the puppy down the busy street. We live in the mountains. My dogs don't know what traffic is. Not the girls. The boys grew up in the city, they're trained not to cross a street.

Locking Lena back in the cabin, we hang out for one last beer in Jesse's yard, smoking cigarettes and joints, until Carlin mentions he should get home. His family was expecting him yesterday. They know he's okay, but still.

Taking over at the wheel, I backtrack a full mile to the next freeway entrance so I don't have to turn against traffic, passing Chris' apartment on the way. We could have just taken him home. Actually, it was better this way, not having to carry his drums from the nearby residential neighborhood to his door. Jesse can pull his Suburban within a few yards of Chris' place.

I get out with Carlin in front of his gate and help him get his bag from the lower compartment. "Thanks for everything, bro. Hope you're okay. If you need anything, let me know." We hug and he shuffles alone down the street, toward his house.

"Are we there yet?" Zaya winks at me from the passenger seat, putting her bare feet up on the dash.

"Yep, this is the place, do you like it?" I say, deadpan, waving my hand toward the empty street. It's about another forty-five minutes, I tell her. This is the last point of civilization, I say. "Hope you're ready for the middle of nowhere."

"I'm from the middle of nowhere already." She doesn't know what she's getting herself into. Days and days without seeing or speaking to another human. Except each other, now.

It's dark, so I'll have to give her a tour of the property tomorrow. Tonight, I show her the inside, the studio is the only real highlight. Otherwise, it's pretty much just a regular house. Scooping out two heaping bowls of rocky road, I pour milk into one and stir to make a thick paste.

"Me, too," she says, and I pour milk into the other bowl before shoving the carton back into the fridge and leading her upstairs.

In bed, we watch episodes of Community while eating ice cream and chocolate donuts. It feels good to laugh with someone. I've seen these episodes at least four or five times each, as with most of the shows I watch. It's a security-blanket kind of thing. This is the first time I've laughed out loud at them. I set the timer on the TV and pull the three layers of blankets up to my neck. I don't know how long I sleep. It seems like forever. Could be days. I smell breakfast when I wake up.

Acknowledgements

To my real-life band mates, B (Carlin) & Chris (Lawrch), thanks for your contribution to the music, support, and allowing me to use you as inspiration for the characters in this story.

Katie, thank you for all of your support throughout all of my writing projects.

To all those who inspired this story, but will never need it: Acknowledge.

My playlist while writing this includes Reel Big Fish, 80's cartoon intros, Simon Whistler videos and Community episodes. And for the second edition, Steely Dan, Lionel, Christopher Cross, Boz Scaggs, Kenny Loggins – and sometimes Messina.

The story *might* be fiction, but the music is real. Listen to or download The Walls Instead album, Rockstar Nobody, for free on YouTube.

See you on the next tour.

Tweed Jefferson

Crepuscular, Certified "Weird Kid", The Man Behind the Curtain

Tweed is an author (obviously). He's also a black belt in some Japanese martial arts, plays a silly number of instruments, and likes to make things – from custom arcade machines to hand-carved guitars. After writing a bunch of books during quarantine, he decided to go back to school to study zoology.

Tweed has over two decades of experience in music production and publishing. He spent the same twenty-some years earning a 'real' living as a web and graphic designer. These experiences come together in several of his books, such as his time on tour and in the studio being used as fodder for both the **Rockstar Nobody** series and his non-fiction book about how to be a DIY musician. As the Executive Editor at Squill Publishing, he lends his knowledge and skills to up-and-coming authors and artists.

Not the opposite of life,
just part of it.

squillpublishing.com

www.ingramcontent.com/pod-product-compliance
Lightning Source LLC
LaVergne TN
LVHW090528110826
845146LV00003B/1024
* 9 7 9 8 9 8 9 8 0 0 5 2 0 *